IN LOVE WITH A CHI-TOWN STEPPER

YASAUNI

Cole Hart
SIGNATURE NOVELS

In Love With A Chi-Town Stepper

Published in the United States of America.

Published by Cole Hart Signature, LLC.

Mailing List

To stay up to date on new releases, plus get information on contests, sneak peeks, and more,

Go To The Website Below...

www.colehartsignature.com

ACKNOWLEDGMENTS

First, I want to thank God because without him I don't know where I would be. I would like to thank my mother, Debra for understanding when I can't do everything, she wants me to do because I'm writing. I have to thank my homie Veto for being there for me listening to my ideas and giving me advice and ideas when needed. Tina, man you have become more like a sister. You are always sound reasoning in my life and with my books, I love you. I know I'm probably missing a lot of people but never charge it to my heart. To my readers I can't thank you all enough for the support.

Facebook: Yasauni Mc
Instagram: Yasauni
Twitter: Yasauni McWilliams@sauniD

I dedicate this book to my uncles that has left us too soon. David, Lawrence, Floyd, and Clarence you all are missed more than you know.

PROLOGUE

ISRAEL

The slight breeze moved the bushes that I hid behind while waiting for my connect to show up. I had been crouched down for so long that my legs were going numb, but I couldn't let this once in a lifetime opportunity pass me by. I had worked so hard trying to pull my life together after coming up from having nothing. I knew what I was sitting here about to do wasn't right, but this nigga had fucked me over one too many times. Every time I reupped with him the weight was off. For a whole year I hadn't said anything; he never gotten one complaint out of me. I had my reasons though; I knew it would all come down to this day. I kept my head down and kept flipping my shit until he trusted me enough to let me get something big from him.

I smirked thinking about all the money I had lost along the way to this nigga that I was about to get back ten-fold today. I wasn't the type of nigga to fuck over people, but if you fucked me over, I didn't care if it took me years to get you back, I was going to get your ass when you least expected. Today was this nigga Curtis' day, and I was itching to get my just do. Yeah, it was fucked up that I was robbing the plug, but what was even more fucked up was for him to get over on a nickel and dime hustler like myself.

I'm a young lil nigga and probably have a few screws loose to be doing this, but who the hell wants to stand on the block and hustle only to make little to nothing? I am the youngest nigga on the block but the only one that sees the bigger picture. Some of these niggas out here happy just to be able to buy the next pair of new Jordon's that come out. I wasn't that person though. I planned on becoming a millionaire before I turned twenty-five. So, I saved every dime I could to flip something larger each time I went back to him. I played my role and kept shit a buck with him until he trusted me enough to do this deal today. I was supposed to be get fronted five kilos, but little did Curtis know, I was about to get that shit for free. It took hard work and dedication to get to this point. I had followed this nigga for months watching his every move until I could pinpoint where he was at any time of the day.

This is where people went wrong at, they kept a daily routine without switching it up. I looked at my watch. I had about a good three minutes before he pulled up with the same two duffle bags that he always carried with him into the same building at the same time every Tuesday. The air began to get thick with humidity as the wind picked up a little; the once clear sky turned full of dark clouds, and out of nowhere, the first big drop of rain fell, hitting my face. The rain came rushing out of the sky, calming the storm of nerves inside of me.

Several times within these last few hours I had told myself I couldn't and shouldn't do this, but the more I thought about how this nigga tried to get down on me, I knew I had to. Plus, I had a mother and sister that I had to take care of because my pops was nowhere around. Also, I wanted to take my brothers in the hood to another level. I refused for us to be out here hustling making the next nigga rich. I wasn't just out here for myself. I was out here for everybody that had helped me along the way.

When the headlights to the car approaching came to a stop,

I took a few deep breaths and waited for the door to open. Curtis was the type of man that didn't trust anyone so when he made stops like this, he was always by himself. He sat in the car for a minute before he opened the door and one of his expensive ass leather shoes hit the pavement then the other. He stood from the car and checked his surrounding like he always did before walking to the door of the building that was set up like a printing business. He turned his back to where I hid and took several steps towards the door before I put the cold piece of steel to the back of his head.

"I'm sure you have no idea who you're robbing right now, so I'll let you slide if you walk away right now." I surprised myself with the manic laugh that left me

"Yeah, you want to overlook me putting a gun to your head like I overlooked you skimming off of me," I told him with venom in my voice.

"Who the fuck are you?" he asked aggressively. I shook my head. The nigga had gotten over on so many people that he had no idea who was behind him. I had come to him once a week for over a year and he still didn't recognize my voice; he deserved to be robbed. I laughed and he tried to turn around again, but I pushed the gun harder into his head.

"Israel?" he questioned shockingly. Yes, it was me, the nigga people least expected because I was the youngest nigga selling work and probably the dumbest for robbing this nigga.

. . .

"Drop the fucking bags and leave the questions to a minimum, and I might think about letting you walk away from this." I lied smoothly. The moment I decided to do this was the moment I decided to off this grimy ass muthafucka. People in the hood took young people like me as a joke, after this, the joke definitely would be on them. He finally dropped the bags at his feet.

"I thought we were friends?" he asked, and I laughed.

"If you treat your friends like you've treated me, I would hate to be your enemy," I told him and pulled the trigger three times once in his head and twice in his back. He dropped to the ground and the heavy rain washed his blood down the nearby drain. I picked up the bags and ran to my car, never looking back.

I walked into the trap house soaked from the rain and dropped both bags on the table.

"What's all this?" one of my boys asked me before I opened the bags.

"This is how we eat," I told them, dumping ten kilos of coke on the table.

I

ISRAEL

"Come on, bro. Let me explain." My nose flared as I watched the nigga from the block stutter about why my money was short. Shit, it was past short; it was damn near invisible. My right-hand man Trig stood next to me with a lethal expression that only he could perfect with his dessert eagle pointed at him. I hated when shit like this went down, but me being who I am, I couldn't let the smallest thing slip through the cracks. I considered myself a fair leader, but all of that went out the window when you disrespected me. My count being off was total disrespect, and I wasn't going to allow no nigga that privilege, even the one standing in front of me.

"Explain to me how I put you on the block to put money in your pocket and feed your family and you forget to pay the man that's helping you eat." I waited for an explanation but Trig holding a gun on him had him shook. Everybody that knew the nigga knew he was a loose ass cannon. I understood it, but I should have been his main focus. I cut my eyes at Trig and he lowered his gun.

"Okay, talk to me and I'll talk back," I told him, snapping my fingers in front of him to get his attention. His eyes finally met mine and piss ran down his legs. Although my voice was calm and my demeanor was relaxed, my eyes said it all. All I wanted was the money that he owed me. Anything he said and did other than digging in his fucking pockets was irrelevant.

It had been ten years since I put the hood on, ten years to get my people where we wanted to be. Shit had been hard, but we built a fucking empire. I wasn't about to let a lying, cheating ass motherfucka destroy my business. From the way he was standing in front of me now, I knew if the police got his ass, he would tell them everything they wanted to know. He wasn't about to leave this alley either way it went, but a dead man couldn't pay his debt.

"Strip," I told that nigga, knowing he had my money somewhere on him.

"Huh."

"Don't huh me motherfucka! Take that shit off, and I mean everything." The tone of my voice changed, and he jumped before he turned his pockets inside out then started taking off his clothes. I shook my head when he kicked off his fresh pair of Jordan's that came out today. When he got to his socks, he stopped, and I pointed to his feet. He pulled off his socks and money started falling to the ground. I shook my head at him. He bent down and picked it up then pulled up the insoles to his shoes and handed me the other money. I eyed it, still seeing that it was short, but it would have to do. He began to put his wet ass clothes back on and as soon as he stepped his feet into his shoes and looked at me, I turned to walk away when a gun went off behind me.

To some people, it was ruthless, but to me it was just business. I could have let it go but letting one slide, you'll then have an army going against you. I had worked too hard to rise to the top to let something like that happen. The hood was finally in a place where we could soon sit back and let our money make itself. I was happy that everything I wanted from the beginning was within arm's reach by the time I was twenty-five years old, and I was damn near ready to give all this up and reap the fruits of my labor. It was only one thing stopping me. I might have been the nutcase that robbed the plug, but me and my brothers built a dynasty off this shit. I couldn't pass the torch right now if I wanted to; no one was going to treat my people like I did. Some of the things we did was heartless, but in retrospect, I have a big ass heart.

As soon as I got to the car, I turned my fifth of Remi XO up to my lips, taking a large gulp. At twenty-five I had plenty of demons, but I let the spirits at the bottom of the bottle take them away. When Trig got in the car, I looked at him and shook my head.

"What?" He asked. I just shook my head nothing to him and he smirked at me.

"You know the rule, if you pull that muthafucka out, you better use it." He told me shrugging. That was the very first rule he gave me when I hit these streets. I lived by that rule and it had saved my life more times than I could count. I put the Remi back up to my mouth because that was the only way I knew how to cope. Ten years living the life that I was living seemed like a lifetime. I had more problems than I could handle and being the one that paid everybody at the end of the week made it even worse.

"You good?" Trig asked as we pulled off to head to a meeting that we were late for. The nigga killed me with the two worded conversations and questions, but that's just who he was, a man of little to no words. He took me under his wing when I was out here wildin and taught me how to survive on these streets. I would always look up to him like a brother because he understood when my mother didn't. When I was out here being dumb, I felt like I had nothing to lose so I did what I wanted, but I didn't learn how to survive out here until he stepped in. He taught me how to get money; it didn't matter if it was selling a pack on the streets or robbing the next nigga. A mutual respect for each other turned into brotherly love and we built an unbreakable bond. If no one else in this world had my back I knew he did, and I stand on that shit.

"I'm good," I told him, hitting the bottle again trying to bury the ghost that was starting to haunt me.

"It's about time y'all made it here," Ziyah said as we opened the door to our main office with her arms folded over her chest. She was the only female in our crew and the only one that we allowed a pass on talking shit to us. She knew her limits, but it didn't stop her from testing the boundaries at times.

"It ain't like we missed shit, don't shit start until I get here anyway," I told her letting my eyes roam over her slim thick frame and my dick jumped. The liquor was in full effect and I was ready to say fuck this meeting, put everybody out, and bend her ass over the table. I knew better though; it was business before I thought of anything pleasurable.

"Sit yo stud looking ass down so we can get this shit over with," I told Ziyah after taking my seat at the head of the table. I loved talking shit to her. She flipped her middle finger up at me and rolled her eyes before sitting her fine ass in her seat. It was a total of six of us Bones, Draco, Lucky, Trig, Ziyah, and me. Everyone at this table moved more bricks in a week than most people seen in a month. Except Ziyah, her hands never touched coke, she only sold weed.

I listened as everyone told me their numbers for the month; everything seemed to add up, so I collected my money and cut shit short.

"Ziyah, let me holla at you for minute," I told her as the room was clearing. She acted like she had an attitude staying behind, but we both knew what it was. Ziyah was my best kept secret and the only rule I have broken. I never mixed business with pleasure, but she was the exception. It wasn't love between us; it was an understanding. We took care of each other's sexual needs and it was back to business as usual. I went to the door, locking it, and before I could walk back to her, she was on her knees in front of me. When her warm mouth wrapped around my dick all I could do was inhale a breath as she bobbed her head up and down on me.

"Fuck," I said when she tried to take me to the back of her throat, she gagged a little and that just turned my freaky ass on more. I grabbed her by the back of her head pushing her mouth further down on me trying to make her take every inch of me. She backed up and that was cool because what I really wanted was pussy anyway. When she stood up, I backed her up to the table and she started stripping out of her clothes. I stood back to appreciate every curve of her chocolate complexion. She was pretty and what I liked about her even more was she didn't give a damn what people thought about her. She was the realest bitch I knew and was down for anything when it came to taking care of business in these streets. She was the type of bitch if I gave her the gun, she was tucking that shit and moving around. We never had to worry about females getting out of order because she was sending hoes to the hospital for little to nothing.

She could make a nigga happy one day, but not me. She wasn't my type, but she had a bomb between her legs and until she told me we couldn't fuck anymore, I was going to be a nigga and do me. To think that shit sounded horrible, but she knew what it was before I stuck my dick in her. I would never lead a bitch on, I wasn't that type of nigga. I had too much to lose and the last thing I wanted to do was kill a bitch. I wasn't opposed to doing the shit, but I don't want to have to, so I make shit clear before I stick my dick in females.

I pulled the magnum over my manhood before I pushed Ziyah on her back on the table. I pulled her ass closer to me and plowed into her. Her moans filled the air, causing me to slam into her again. My next stroke into her was slower and longer and I repeated the action, hitting her spot, making her come back-to-back. When I figured we had been in here long enough,

I stopped playing and got mines off. I sat in the chair behind me as she got up and went into the bathroom. I shook my head thinking one day this shit would change and maybe I would consider having a woman of my own. I chased the thought to the back of my mind because at this point, the only thing I needed in my life was money. The game I played was complicated enough without adding the extra stress of a woman. I got up out the chair not waiting for Ziyah to come out the bathroom before I left.

2

RILEY

B*eep! Beep! Beep!* I groaned, picking up my iPhone and cutting off the alarm with my eyes still closed. All I wanted to do was go back to sleep and enjoy the peace of being in a state that nothing bothered me. I popped my eyes open, knowing that I only had about an hour before everything went to hell. Yeah, hell was the perfect word to describe why at twenty-eight years old I was living this way. I sat up on the side of the bed, turning on my lamp on the nightstand. I grabbed the weed that sat there and rolled up going over the things I had to do in my head. Flaming up I inhaled the smoke; this was the only thing that helped me get through my day without killing a motherfucka and God knows I was ready to off this nigga every time I walked into his room.

"Ri."

This can't be life! I thought to myself as my name was being called over the baby monitor that I left in Curtis' room. All I wanted to do was enjoy my blunt and a shower before I had to be somebody's caregiver. I rolled my eyes, hitting my blunt again because I wasn't about to let him ruin the only peace I had while I was woke. This was my time, and I wasn't about to let him fuck up my time, he had already fucked up my life, ten years of it to be exact. I shook my head because I used to pride myself on being loyal. When this first started, I thought I could do this. The more time that passed it only had let me know that I can't take care of him. I have sacrificed so much of my life to take care of my husband only for him to turn out cruel. I was young as hell when I married Curtis, it wasn't shit anybody could tell me about him. He was every bitch in my neighborhood dream nigga; he had it all. The looks, the money, and he came off as being a gentleman. He was eleven years older than me and did things for me that no one had took out the time to do. I was young and dumb. I married him at eighteen because I thought he loved me. I should've known better though; I was the prettiest girl in the hood that hadn't been touched.

The love I thought that he had for me was nothing but appreciation for a pretty face and a thick ass body that I had let go of over the years. I couldn't even look in the mirror because I was ashamed of my reflection. I stared at my five-carat diamond ring that sat on the nightstand because I would never put it back on my finger. Besides Curtis being fine as hell, this was the type of shit that caught my attention back then. I loved shiny new shit. It wasn't like I had a horrible life at home. I just wanted better, and at that time, Curtis could give me better. He was that nigga in the streets. Once he approached me, I was ready to be his ride or die. Not one motherfucka could tell me what I was feeling wasn't love.

"Ri bitch you hear me!" his harsh voice came over the speaker again only for me to ignore him again. Every morning when I woke up, I was hoping that nigga was dead and sometimes I was so close to finishing the job that someone else started. Most times I found myself asking God why that shot to the head only grazed him. I wanted nothing more than to leave his ass, most times I just wanted to end him, but I couldn't. I was a loyal ass woman, I finished smoking my blunt and went to the shower to get dressed for the day.

I stepped back into my room only to hear Curtis yelling and

calling me every name in the book he could think of. I slipped on a pair of jogging pants and an oversized t-shirt, that had become my daily uniform. I walked to Curtis door and took a deep breath. Before opening it, I plastered on a smile trying to keep a good face in front of him but the scowl he wore made it impossible. I let my smile drop and rolled my eyes at him.

"What the fuck is this shit good for if yo ass gone act like you deaf?" He threw the monitor at me, and I dodged it. I stared down at the broken monitor on the floor then back at him.

"Good morning to you too," I told him dryly. When I got married, I hadn't signed up for this shit, but I was married to him, and I took what I said before God and all those ugly ass folks I barely knew to heart. They said in sickness and in health through the good and the bad, until death do us part, and I was trying so hard to keep my vows, but I just didn't know how long I could do it. *I wish this motherfucka would just die already.* I thought to myself then shook it off. I remembered my father's words on the day I married Curtis as I walked slowly towards the bed. *All you have is your word; marrying a nigga like him that's all that matters, loyalty means more than your next breath.*

If I had pushed the wedding back six months, I could have avoided all of this. That's all I had of being a happy wife, six months. After that I became everything he needed like a nurturer, a nurse, a doctor, now his fucking slave and this shit was doing something to me. It had caused me to die inside. I had already lost the small number of friends I had. My father had died, and my mother was out living her best life. She was really the only person I had left, and she was determined to let me learn about life on my own. She was against me marrying Curtis, and I guess it was because she saw something I didn't. I hadn't wanted to hear nothing she had to say concerning him and me. After talking to me so much she let me fall deeper in lust with him. To be honest it wasn't anything she could do or say to keep me away from him. I wanted what I wanted. Now I wished I could give it back.

"What's fucking good about this morning? I can't walk, I can't do shit for myself, everybody done gave up on me, I'm wet, and married to a dumb ass deaf bitch." His words would be comical if I wasn't the dumb ass deaf bitch. I walked closer to him, holding the back of my neck to keep from putting my hands on him.

"What the fuck you standing there for? Help me bitch." I cocked my head at him because I was fed up.

"Your diapers are over there in the corner and your wheelchair is five feet to the right, get up and do this shit yourself." I smirked and walked out of the room. That nigga had blown my high and I knew I couldn't take any more of his antics without being high as hell.

I walked back into my room, grabbed my keys and left the house. As I drove away, I looked in my rearview mirror. I had the biggest, prettiest house on the block. Too bad all it was filled with was pain and anger. I pulled up to the store to grab some honey dutch blunts and whatever else I would need for the day. I was so lost in my thoughts that I hadn't saw the man in front of me until I damn near knocked him over. Or maybe I was the one that was falling because he wrapped his strong arms around me and pulled me into his solid chest.

I kept my eyes closed tight as I inhaled his scent and enjoyed being in a man's arms even if it was just by accident. I hadn't felt this feeling in so long I just wanted to stay there and never go back to the hell I had been in for so long. His grip was strong yet gentle as he stood me up on my feet. I finally pulled my head back from his chest and slowly looked up into his slanted chocolate eyes and was lost. The shit that I was feeling just staring at him was the type of shit you saw only in movies. The butterflies in my stomach fluttered like nothing I had felt before. It felt like I had been knowing this stranger all my life because the only thing that went through my head was *you're safe*. He looked down at me, and his eyes seemed to speak to me before he could open his mouth. I searched his expression, I could tell that he seemed to be tired, but I intrigued him. I finally broke our gaze, but he kept his arms around me, and I was able to really look at him. I took in his pecan complexion, his full kissable lips, his crisp lining, and curly jet-black hair.

Was it possible for a nigga to be pretty? I thought to myself. I was just about to step back when I felt his dick get hard on my hip and grow down both of our legs. My mouth parted just a little as I looked back into his eyes. There was no shame in them as he smirked at me and kind of shook his leg to readjust himself. *All that dick I had just felt it was going to take more than a leg shake to readjust that.* I smirked back at him and stepped back but I couldn't keep my eyes from falling below his belt line.

"You good, Pressure?" His deep voice didn't match the face I was staring into. I looked around when he spoke to see who he was talking to, but I noticed he was still looking down at me. I raised my eyebrow at him like he was losing his mind. I wasn't about to correct his sexy ass though.

"Yeah," I replied, still staring at him trying to keep myself from fucking him right here, right now. My pussy was pulsating to be touched by him, and at this point, she had a mind of her own and was ready for anything. He licked his lips, causing me to bite down on my own lip to keep from telling him let me lick that muthafucka for him. In a matter of seconds, I pictured all the nasty shit I could do to him that some nigga robbed me of for the last ten years.

I cocked my head at him trying to figure out what was going on. We had been standing in this aisle for what seemed like forever talking to each other without saying a word. This was something that had never happened to me before, not even with my husband. I was twenty-eight years old and didn't even know what it was like to live without taking care of someone. I didn't know what it felt like to be touched in the way that this man had touched me; it wasn't even in an intimate way. In my mind, this man had fucked me forty ways from Friday and I wanted him to do just that.

I cleared my throat and finally stepped back, bringing myself out of the illusion he had me entranced in.

"My bad," I told him and smiled a little, turning my back to him.

"That's it?" his deep ass voice cut through my thoughts of taking him down in this store and not giving a fuck who saw us. I turned to him, raising my eyebrow questioningly at him.

"What's the problem?" I asked him, trying to divert my eyes everywhere but on him. It didn't work because his presence demanded my attention.

"You just gone knock me over, use me to hold you like that nigga you fuck with won't, then eye fuck me until you came, and walk away? I can't get your name or number?" I smirked at him, shaking my head no.

"That's some typical nigga shit, I feel used." He said, laughing. He was right I had eye fucked him, but I didn't come until he smiled at me. *Fuck my life! This nigga was sexy as hell.* I thought to myself as I saw his dimples wink at me. I stared at him for a minute and wondered how he knew what I wasn't getting at home.

For the first time in a long time, I looked down at myself and became self-conscious about my appearance. My hair was in a messy bun, and I was out here at the end of spring in an oversized jogging suit to hide the twenty pounds I had put on over the years added to my already thick frame. Here he was standing in front of me looking like God had dropped his perfect ass on earth and left him here for women like me to gush over. I wanted to let my eyes roam over him one more time before I walked away, but I was too embarrassed to stand in front of him any longer.

I turned on my heels quick only to damn near fall over my own feet.

"I got you," he told me as he kept me upright, steadying me again. The way he said it did something to me, it was like it had more meaning than it should have coming from a total stranger.

"Thank you!" I told him, straightening my clothes and looking down at my feet. If I wasn't embarrassed before, I was definitely embarrassed now.

"Why the solemn look? Don't be embarrassed; shit happens Pressure." He told me. I nodded my head and walked in the opposite direction he was facing. I hurried to the counter to pay for the little stuff I had gotten. I handed the cashier a twenty and she shook her head no to me.

"The guy with the sexy smile gave me money for your things already, he told me to tell you he got you." She smiled at me like it was the sweetest thing in the world. I gave her a smile and nodded my head, accepting the excessive amount of money he left. The nigga was a real charmer, but he could keep his money.

I was past the stage in life where money made me happy, all I wanted was people that was real and loyal.

As I drove home, I thought about the guy in the store and the way he smiled at me as I smoked my blunt. When I pulled into the garage, I sat there for a long time thinking about my life. I had wasted so much time trying to be loyal to a person that I never loved because fucking with a nigga in the streets required loyalty. I dreaded every minute that I was awake in this house. Everything seemed so dark because of all the negative energy Curtis put in the air. When he found out he wasn't going to be able to walk again, I went from being called boo, baby, and ma, to hoe, bitch, and slut.

I thought about dude in the store again, he had a swag about him that I had never saw in a man before. *Pressure* I heard his voice in my head as I thought of the name he gave me. The shit would've been weird to me if any other nigga would have donned me with that name. But he had a way of saying it, that made my pussy wet. I exhaled a breath, knowing I would never see him again and life as I knew was about to continue. As I walked to the door of the house, I heard Curtis yelling like someone was killing him, and all thoughts of the fine ass man in the store became a distant memory.

3

ISRAEL

"Damn, baby; you going crazy." I closed my eyes as Ziyah sucked my dick like she had something to prove. This was the first time I had a chance to sit down in a couple days and what better way to relax than getting some head. I opened my eyes in time to see her spit on my dick and go back down to clean it up. *She must want something* the thought crossed my mind when she looked me in my eyes coming back up to the tip. In my line of work, every time you turned around somebody wanted something from you. Normally they had their hand out for some money, but I could tell she wanted something else, something I knew I wouldn't be able to give her. I saw everything she was feeling in her eyes, if nothing else I could read people and she was showing her hand. Ziyah was cool enough to fuck, and cool enough to sell my weed, but she was like any other female that came around me. Ziyah wanted the crown and everything that came with fucking with a nigga like me.

This shit was my fault, an occasional bend over the table after a meeting had turned into her being at my local condo bobbing on my dick and busting it open for a real nigga at least three times a week. The only good thing about this was that nobody knew we were fucking around.

I pushed her head down and closed my eyes acting like what she was doing was just the best feeling in the world to me. If I was being truthful about it I did it to avoid her, my dick hadn't gotten soft, but I wasn't as into it as I was before. A vision of the woman that ran into me at the store came to my mind and I felt my dick get harder. I imagined her nutmeg complexion and messy ass ponytail in her head. She had doe-shaped chestnut brown eyes with thick eyebrows and a bow-shaped mouth. Her lips were full but not overly big and she stood about five feet six inches. Even with the baggy jogging pants and T-shirt on, she was shapely enough for me to see some of her curves, but nothing was better than feeling the curve of her waist when she bumped into me. She was the kind of thick that I loved; big breasts, hippy with the thighs to match, and a flat stomach. She was at the store looking a hot ass mess, but it didn't take away from her smooth, pretty face and beautiful smile. I pictured her on her knees in front of me and in no time, I felt the tingle in my nuts letting me know I was close to coming in her mouth.

I grabbed the back of Ziyah head and help her get me to a place I rarely got with her giving me head. When Ziyah began to stop me from pushing her mouth down on me, I began to fuck her mouth. I had been playing shit cool with Ziyah. I was really a freaky nigga that liked to do freaky shit, but I held back with her. I fucked Ziyah's mouth without her protesting until I released in her mouth. I pulled out of her mouth and she looked at me in disgust spitting my nut on the floor.

"What the fuck is wrong with you Iss? You know I hate that shit the fuck." She shortened my name I watched her get off her knees and she rolled her eyes at me.

"How you want to sit on the throne and be the queen if you can't accept my kids?" I asked her with a smirk on my face. Ziyah stared at me like I was one of those soft ass niggas she used to fuck with.

"So, you saying I have to swallow your nasty ass nut to fuck with you on some real shit?" she asked me with her face balled up. Her face said one thing, but I can see her brain at work; it amazed me what I could get these bitches to do. Females like her would go from Jewish to Baptist if it gave them a chance with me. I shook my head at her getting off the couch reaching for my phone. It had been blowing up since she put her mouth on me and I needed to see what was going on. I looked at my phone and smiled when I saw it was my little sister Aubrey, I hit her name to return her call and Ziyah was still standing in the middle of the floor like she was glued in place. I looked at her from her Jordan covered feet to her face then settled on her eyes.

"Get that shit off my floor," I told her and went into my room to get dressed.

"What up Brey?" I asked my little sister who wasn't as little as I wanted her to be anymore. She was damn near a grown woman, eighteen years old, and one of the two women that held my heart. I put the phone on speaker so I could move around the room as I listened to her.

"What's up Bro, you coming to the house today?" she asked and if she was asking, she wanted something. Aubrey and my mother Shawn were the only two women that I allowed to stay deep in my pockets. I was doing this shit for them, and they could have whatever they wanted from me.

"I'll be there in a minute," I replied, hanging the phone up so I could get ready. Before I got in the shower, I heard my front door closed but went out to see if Ziyah really left. I hopped in the shower, got dressed, and grabbed the gifts that I had gotten last week for my mom and sister before heading out.

"Ma... Ma!" I yelled for my mother as I walked in the door.

"Ma!" I yelled again, knowing I was getting on her nerves and that's why she hadn't answered me. She hated when Aubrey and I yelled through the house and even being grown as hell, we still did it just to get under her skin.

"Stop fucking yelling through my house like you crazy." When I heard her voice coming from the kitchen I laughed and walked in that direction. When I got in there, she gave me that look that made me sit my ass down like a kid. I laughed, kissing her on the cheek but not after I gave her a side-eye. She smacked the back of my head and pointed to the chair for me to sit down.

"You and Brey get on my nerves with that shit; one day I'm a fuck y'all up." I smiled at her and drummed my fingers on the table.

"What you been up too?" I asked her as she dropped a chicken wing in the hot grease and sizzling filled the air with an aroma that took my mind back to when we were living in the projects on the low end. We had come a long way from me hiding crack and guns in a small ass concrete box that we called an apartment. My mother deserved everything I got her and more, she had worked three jobs just to make it out of the projects and bought her own house when I was thirteen. I respected her for doing that just to make our life better, but by then she had lost me to the streets. She was working to give us a better chance at life, and I was hitting the block to make sure me and my sister had the best clothes and shit. I was young as hell making runs for the niggas that sold drugs. I barely made it out of eighth grade and never graduated high school, but the next nigga could never tell. I was naturally smart, but more than that, I was a fucking street genius and that was my biggest gift and worse curse. I'll never forget when my mother kicked me out of this very house for finding a gun I thought I had hidden well. I didn't agree with the shit at the time, but her actions turned me into the man and beast I am today. I didn't buy my mother's house but with the first real money I came into I made sure her shit was paid off. She was able to cut out two of three jobs that she worked, and I made sure the money she made stayed in her pocket.

I took care of her now and I have always taken care of Brey, it was nothing the ladies in my life couldn't ask for and get.

"The same shit different day," was my mother's reply, and I laughed a little.

"Trying to keep your fast ass little sister away from these niggas she be talking to. I'm actually glad you came over because we need to talk to you about some things." I raised my eyebrow at her. I hadn't heard the last thing she said after Brey and niggas.

"Aubrey Lynette Carson, get yo ass down here now." I had walked away from my mother to the steps yelling for Brey. Somebody in this house had shit fucked up if they thought I was just going to let all this go down. I closed my eyes to calm down because Aubrey was going to have me out here killing these little boys over her. She acted like she hadn't listened to anything I had taught her over the years. *Fuck these lil boys, get an education, and boss up on these niggas. There ain't a female I don't know that doesn't want to be a boss in her own right. The only way to do that is to be smart, get those degrees under your belt and nobody can tell you shit.* I thought about the words I had told her so many times and she was out here chasing dick. I had to calm myself down, all her life I had never put my hands on her, but I was ready to choke the shit out this little girl.

"Why you calling me like you crazy?" Brey asked when she got to the bottom of the stairs. I stepped back staring at her, she had on a pair of blue jean shorts that looked like a pair of panties, with a shirt that barely covered her bra, her weave hung to her ass, and when I saw the sparkle that came from her navel, I almost lost my mind. My nose flared and I bit down on my fist to keep from punching the fucking wall.

"Is that makeup on your face?" I asked her and she nodded. I just walked off before I flipped the fuck out in this house.

Aubrey followed behind me talking shit, but I wasn't trying

to hear anything she was saying. I needed to collect my thoughts, Brey was growing into a woman and I wasn't ready for it. I couldn't beat her ass and I couldn't kill every nigga that came her way as much as I may have wanted to. All I could do was give her the game and hope she was a quick study, because any nigga that broke her heart was going to deal with me.

I went in my pocket and pulled out the box that I had for her and slid it across the kitchen table to her. She smiled at me and it made me happy to make her happy. She didn't know what was in the box, but she was happy to get a gift. When she opened it, her face lit up like the Chicago skyline at night. She took out the ten-carat tennis bracelet and the gleam in her eyes sparkled brighter than the diamonds she was now holding in her hands. She got out of her chair and ran around the table to give me a hug.

"Thank you!" she kissed my cheek and got ready to leave the kitchen.

"Naw come back here," I told her and she turned staring at me like I had two heads, but she walked slowly back to her chair, sitting down.

"Ma told me you out here fucking with these niggas." She began to shake her head at me, but I held up my hand to cut her off. If she was, she wasn't going to tell me. I didn't want to hear her truths or her lies.

"I know you getting older and about to start all that girly shit y'all be getting into. You're starting to show interest in the lil niggas around you. I get all that Brey, but you have to be smart about whatever you do." she nodded her head at me.

"Don't just nod at me Brey! Understand that you deserve more than the boys you are interested in will be willing to give. I would tell you don't fuck with nobody that can't do what I do for you. Being realistic about it, most niggas can't and the ones that can, I don't want you around. I've always treated you how I want the men that you would one day fuck with should treat you."

"What buying me gifts doing the things to keep a smile on

my face?" she asked, and I nodded my head.

"That's a part of it, but the biggest thing I have always done is treated you with respect and loved you. If them lil niggas you fucking with ain't going to do that, then you need to move around. If you have to question it, it ain't real and if you have trouble the first thing you do is call me. Don't be out here just giving away the goods either," I told her.

"The goods?" She questioned with a frown on her face.

"Yeah, pussy," I told her only for my mother to smack the back of my head. My conversation with Aubrey was over. I only hoped that she took what I said and ran with it. I know how things go at that age. When I was her age, I had my share of girls that would do anything to fuck with a nigga of my caliber. I just hoped she took in the things that I had showed her and taught her as she was growing up. Brey was five years younger than me, and I protected her from a lot of things that I got into.

One thing that I never hid or lied about was what bitches would do to fuck with a nigga like me. I did the best I could with her, I couldn't be the father figure she needed because I never had one myself. I figure I taught her enough to stand on her own when the time came and evidently that time was now. I made a mental note to put a tail on her because at this point, I would have to watch her ass like a hawk. She wouldn't be out here like her little friends and I was going to make sure of that even if I had to have a muthafucka trunk her little ass every now and then to prove a point to her. I wasn't above invading her privacy if it kept her safe and out of harm's way.

"I hate that fucking word," she said after hitting me. I walked over to the stove and grabbed a couple pieces of chicken, putting them on a plate. I went into my back pants pocket and handed my mother an envelope.

"I'll be back in a couple of days and we can have the talk you wanted."

"Okay son." She told me and tossed the envelope on the counter.

4
RILEY

I smiled as Curtis cursed me out and called me all types of bitches as I wheeled his raggedy ass into the worse nursing home I could find in the city. I was about to take my life back and I was about to show him that shit could be way worse than what he thought it was. The days after meeting that fine ass man in the store I realized I was selling myself short staying with Curtis. It was time that I be loyal to myself and start to live, I needed to find myself. I didn't even know who I was anymore and that was fucking with my head. I wasn't put on this earth to take care of an ungrateful ass man.

I refused to live like this, I refused to be held back, I refused to be any fucking body's doormat. It was things out here that women needed like peace, happiness, friends, and love. I wanted all those things plus more. I wanted to travel and see the world and I couldn't do that if I stayed with him. I already had my bags packed and got everything that was in the safe out and divided it between us. I only took half the money we had in our joint bank account and left the rest for him. To be honest I deserved all that shit.

Once I signed his ass over, I was going straight to the airport. The house was already on the market for little to nothing and all of his businesses was still in his name except the funeral home. I was keeping that because until I figure out what I wanted to do, I needed an income. My divorce papers were signed, and I didn't take any of the other property or businesses that he owned. He could keep all that shit as long as I didn't have to deal with his evil ass anymore.

"Bitch I swear I'm a kill you!" Curtis yelled as I wheeled him into the door.

"Let me see you get up out that chair and do it," I told him with a smirk on my face. Hopefully this would be the last time I heard him call me a bitch. At first, it used to bother me, even depress me, now I was having the last laugh. I don't think I would've had the courage to do this to him if he had hadn't smacked the dog shit out of me last week. I had already let him verbally and mentally abuse me, but that smack was like a wakeup call. I wasn't about to allow a crippled muthafucka that I was taking care of to fuck me up. The bruise on my face and part of my eye was just about gone and so was I.

I pushed Curtis into the facility, smiled at the receptionist, and left his ass at the desk. As I walked out, he yelled that he was sorry for how he had treated me. His cries fell on deaf ears because nothing he would say would make me turn back. When he yelled at me, he had taken care of me all these years he was right. Financially, I didn't have to want for shit, but all of it came at a cost. It had cost me ten years that I would never get back, but I was about to start making up for lost time.

Chicago springs had been good, but I heard that the spring was better in Miami, and I was about to find out.

❧

I was sitting on south beach Miami in my cabana looking at the waves crash against the sand drinking my second Mojito of the day. This place was beautiful, and it was so peaceful. I had my laptop in front of me researching schools because I had to do something with my life. Everything nursing was popping up, I knew I would be good at it, but I was tired of taking care of people. I wanted to do something where I could be my own boss, but I had no idea where to start.

"Hey beautiful; do you mind if I keep you company?" I looked up at the man standing in front of me he was cute. He had a Spanish accent, was well built, and at about six feet tall. I let my eyes roam over him taking him in and thought about the fact that I hadn't had the company of a man in a long time. My pussy began to get wet just from looking at him. I felt a smirk creep on my face that turned into a full-blown smile before I spoke.

"Sure." Any other time I would have turned away any man that approached me, but this was a new me. If I wanted to step outside of my box, I had to start somewhere, and fucking a man in Miami would be a good start. In my mind, I could have a sexcapade and wouldn't have to worry about getting in too deep because I would be leaving here in a week.

"My name is Jose," he said with a smile on his face. He had the perfect smile with light brown eyes that seemed like they shined under the sun. I licked my lips because my mouth was starting to water looking at him. I didn't connect to him like I did with the guy in the store a couple of weeks ago, but Jose did a number on me physically. My pussy was speaking its own language to let Jose do some shit to me that had never been done to me before and I was about to let him. The only thing I kept thinking while I was looking at him was yolo. I only had one life to live and I was about to live my best one fucking this man anywhere I pleased.

"Nice to meet you, Jose. I'm Riley, where are you from?" I asked him as he took me in from head to toe. Normally I would recoil because of the weight I had put on, but he seemed to appreciate my curves. His eyes finally moved from my hip area to my eyes, and he smiled.

"Cuba, what about you? You're not from around here." I

smiled and shook my head no and told him I was from Chicago and here on vacation. He nodded his head at me and offered to refill my drink. As he went to go get me another drink, I thought about the fact that I had been here for seven days and really hadn't explored anything. He told me he had lived here for the last five years so I knew he would be able to show me a good time besides in the bedroom. So, when he came back, I asked him about the best clubs and bars to visit and he offered to show me around. After my third drink, we decided that we would meet up later and do a night club tour.

I decided to do a little shopping because going out to the clubs was the last thing, I thought I would be doing, and I needed something to put on for the night. I put on the little jean shorts I had with me and opted to wear my bikini top instead of putting on my oversized tee shirt. I put my large shades on grabbed my bag and hit up the strip.

I walked into the H&M looking down at my phone not paying attention to my surroundings and bam. I bumped into someone dropping my phone out of my hand and nearly hitting the floor. An arm went around my waist keeping me upright and when I looked up to see who saved me, I became embarrassed.

5

ISRAEL

I looked down at the woman that couldn't seem to stay away from me and smirked.

"I'm so—"

"Sorry." I finished her words. If she didn't seem so innocent, I would have thought this bitch was trying to put a hit on me or was the hitman. She was just so oblivious to things like how to walk without knocking people over. I stood her up and took in her body baby girl was showing every inch of her skin in her shorts and bikini top. I knew she would be applying pressure to these bitches once she got out of those big ass joggers. She was so damn pretty and thick as fuck; I was ready to bend her ass over and let everyone in Miami see that she was mines and keep they fucking hands and eyes off her.

"If you gone be following me around you don't have to knock me over every time. Just tell me you want the D and I got you." I watched her face flush and her mouth part just a little before she cleared her throat. I took that opportunity to wrap an arm around her waist and let my hands drop to her ass. I grabbed a handful of her ass pulling her closer to me, I thought she would step back, but shorty came closer rubbing her thigh against my dick. She bit down on her lip, and I pictured it wrapped around my meat, gliding up and down. I instantly got hard; nothing made my dick harder than a woman that knew what she was doing sucking my dick. I had no doubt that shorty could get the job done efficiently.

"I think you're the one following me." She finally spoke, and I smirked at her. She had no idea I could find out exactly who she was, where she lived, who she was fucking, and make him a fucking memory with one phone call, but for some reason, I felt the need to be different with her. She didn't seem like the type to be involved in the shit I was into, usually that was a turn off to me. I needed to utilize anyone that came into my surroundings that wanted to fuck with me, but she was different.

"Naw baby girl. I've never been a follower always a leader." I smirked at her because she had no idea who I was, and I liked it that way.

"What brought you to Miami?" She asked, and I smiled a little.

"Business, you?" I asked, still palming her ass.

"Pleasure," she told me, letting her eyes roam over me.

"Let's just cut the bullshit, you coming with me tonight." She raised her eyebrow at me. None of what I said had a hint of question in it. I told her ass what it was.

"No, I have a prior engagement, but maybe I'll see you around." I looked down at her and smirked, muthafuckas never told me no, and she was letting me down nicely. I smiled because it only made me want her even more.

"Iss, can I get your card to pay for my stuff?" I took a deep breath when I heard Ziyah's voice. That bitch knew she could fuck up a wet dream. I wanted to go the fuck in on her right there, but I didn't want to scare Pressure by showing her that other side of me. For some reason, I didn't want her to see that. Pressure tried to step back but I held on to her tighter and cut my eyes at Ziyah. She smacked her lips and waited with her hand out. I watched her look Pressure up and down then roll her eyes.

"You act like that bitch all that," she said under her breath with her hands still out for my card.

"Bihh!" Part of the word left my mouth before I realized it and reeled it back in. Ziyah had lost her fucking mind, and I was about to help her find her shit quickly.

"Let me take care of this right quick." I bent down and whispered in Pressure's ear, stepping away from her. When my eyes landed on Ziyah, she took a couple of steps back; she knew she had fucked up. I cocked my head at her and collected my thoughts before I opened my mouth. The last thing I wanted was a run in with Miami Dade for choking the shit out of this girl in public.

"Who the fuck you think you talking to?" I asked her, stepping closer to her, lowering my voice. Ziyah's head dropped a little, she wanted to act like a bitch in here, so I was about to treat her like one. I moved a little closer to her and grabbed her wrist, squeezing it just a little. I didn't want to hurt her, but I needed her to understand some things. She twisted her wrist in my grip, and I tightened the hold.

"I didn't mean anything by that, Iss, I was just playing." She stuttered out. I dropped her hand and readjusted my stance in front of her.

"I don't understand how you in here playing the jealous ass girlfriend role when we both know that's not the role you play in my life. We might fuck around every now and then, and have that other little situation going on, but on some real shit, I'm just the nigga you work for. Know your fucking place when it comes to me; if it ain't about money and if I haven't asked you to get on your knees and suck my dick then you shouldn't be saying or doing shit." Ziyah swallowed hard, looking at me like she wanted to cry but fuck her tears. In my eyes, she wanted the same thing that hoes around me wanted from me and I wasn't going for that. I was cautious about everyone around me. It was only a hand full of people I trusted completely, but I only trusted Ziyah with certain things . At first, I trusted her completely, but the longer we fucked around the more complicated everything got with us.

She finally nodded her head at me like she understood where I was coming from.

"I don't expect to have to have this conversation with you again." She nodded her head again. She knew if nothing else I hated to repeat myself. I turned my back to her and looked around for Pressure's sexy ass and she was nowhere in sight. I bit down on my lip pissed off, but at the same time grateful because I really had business to take care of. I looked at the time on my phone and walked out of the door running right into Trig and his girl Honey. They were on time which was nothing less than expected. We waited for Ziyah to get her bags before we got into the car that was waiting for us to meet up with our connect.

After handling our business, we went back to the house we were renting. Business was looking better than ever. I knew if shit continued to look up for us, I would be sitting down by the time I turned thirty. Ten years was a long time to be living the life I was living, and honestly, I was getting tired of the shit I had to deal with. People thought my job was easy because of the fast money, but this life was complicated. Making sure everything runs smoothly was a twenty-four seven job. I had no days off, people thought the trips that I took were for pleasure, but everything I did was business.

"Iss." Ziyah walked out to the pool where I was sitting chilling before Trig and me took her and Honey out tonight. I wasn't really with the shit I wanted to chill at this big ass house I was paying for us to stay in, but I was firm believer in letting muthafuckas enjoy the fruits of their labor. So, we both gave in to the women's request to go out clubbing tonight.

"Unless it's business I don't want to talk about it Ziyah," I told her, not looking in her direction. She stood in front of me with a string bikini on that looked good on her small frame. My eyes roamed from her white polished toes up to her face and I smirked. I knew what she wanted but after how she acted earlier, I wasn't about to pipe her down. She needed to learn her place and the only way I could see her doing that was to stop dicking her down. It was all my fault in the first place. I broke my own rules and now I had to deal with it.

Trig walked out and cleared his throat. Ziyah looked over at him and walked back in the house. The nigga would never know how I was grateful for the small things when it came to him. When he came and sat in a chair away from me, I just looked at him and smiled a little.

"When you gone stop acting like you not fucking that girl?" I laughed because I had never told him what was going on between me and her. I was sure that she talked to Honey, but Honey wasn't the type to take shit back to Trig. That's why I fucked with her hard, she was so much like the nigga that the shit creeped me out at first but her loyalty to the people around her was everlasting.

"Who the hell—" He shook his head cutting me off.

"Nigga I'm trained to see what everyone else doesn't but lately she's been clingy as hell. She even gets a little sparkle in her eyes now when she looks at you." He laughed like the shit was funny. I didn't see the humor in any of it. I wanted to be mad, but this nigga was my day one for a reason; he didn't give a fuck when it came to the truth.

"I'm working on cutting her off. It's just going to take a little time; things like this needs to be done with finesse. I don't want shit coming back to bite me in the ass because I couldn't keep my dick in my pants," I told Trig, thinking about the truth behind me and Ziyah; muthafuckas couldn't know what was really going on. I used to fuck with her hard as hell because she knew her position in my life, but all that shit changed on a drunk night with two simple words, and I've been regretting that shit since then.

My phone rung which it seemed to do constantly. I picked it up and just listened to the person on the other end of the line. I closed my eyes and exhaled a breath before speaking.

"Hold it down. I'll be back in a couple of days," I told one of my workers and picked up the bottle next to me to take a drink, I was too young to have so many problems. I was way too young to be this stressed .If I didn't watch out, my lil ass would die from the shit. Trig looked over at me, waiting for me to say something, but there was no need to get him involved in anything that I could handle myself, so I shook my head at him.

"Let's get ready to go out," I told him standing up with the bottle in my hand walking off.

I sat in the V.I.P. section with Trig and we both were on high alert watching our surroundings. Ziyah and Honey were in the middle of the dance floor having the time of their lives. Trig and I were two niggas from the southside of Chicago and couldn't get comfortable enough in this unknown spot to enjoy ourselves. It wasn't a bad atmosphere; it just wasn't home. I didn't know the layout and I didn't have my pistol on my hip to feel comfortable enough in here. I took a sip of my drink, making sure not to get too fucked up and I let my eyes roam over the crowd for the hundredth time and I couldn't believe this shit.

What were the fucking chances of seeing her again? I stood up and watched her twerk her round fat ass on some Hispanic man and jealousy rose in me. She rolled her body with ease, looking comfortable as he moved his hands over her body. I saw red as I watched him hand her a glass of something, stopping her mid roll and she took a sip from it. She handed it back to him and continued to dance. She didn't seem like the woman I had met on the other occasions; she was loose and smiling. She was feeling herself and was all over this man like she was aching to be touched by him. As she danced, she turned to him and let her hands roam down to her pussy inviting him to something I felt like was mines. I had no right to feel the way I was feeling; by the time he moved his hand to touch the center of her I had made my way to them and snatched her ass back.

The buttons from the blue jean romper she had on popped and her bra was out. I pulled her in to me, picking her up off her feet. I didn't want anyone to see what she had under her clothes but me. For once in my life, I was territorial about someone other than my loved ones. When she looked at me, she smiled and started laughing.

"What the fuck?" the guy she was dancing with asked stepping to me. I cut my eyes at him hoping he would get the hint. I wasn't trying to body a nigga in Miami, but I wasn't opposed to the shit.

"Walk the fuck away," I told him in a lethal tone. Pressure wrapped her arms around my neck and placed her head on my shoulder.

"Iss," she whispered in my ear softly. I diverted my eyes down to her for a hot second because I knew I never told her my name. I thought about our interaction at the mall and knew she heard Ziyah say my name. I turned around to walk out. Trig, Honey, and Ziyah was right behind me. I nodded my head at them, this is exactly why I fucked with them this hard. If one of us moved, we all moved damn near as one. That type of shit was hard to find in friends and I was lucky to have found that in them.

We made it out the door before I heard a voice with a thick Cuban accent yell.

"I haven't gotten her this fucked up so you can take the pussy I was guaranteed tonight." I bent down putting Pressure's high ass in the car and went under the seat, pulling up quick.

"It's too many people out here for that shit right now." Honey spoke under her breath. I dropped the gun that I was holding and turned to dude smiling.

"I normally don't have to speak more than once, but since

you don't know who you fucking with right now I'm a give you a pass. Walk Thee Fuck Away," I told him breaking my words down because evidently this nigga had a problem with his comprehension. I bit down on my bottom lip as he stared at me like he wanted to say something. I nodded my head a couple of times before I swung, clearing him. His back and head hit the pavement with a thud before his snores filled the air.

"Get the fuck in the car!" Ziyah yelled. I jumped in the back seat with Pressure and Honey and Ziyah pulled off before my door was closed. I looked over at Pressure, her eyes were glossy, and she gave me a big ass smile before her head slumped down. I had no idea what that nigga have gave her, but she was out of it within seconds.

"What the fuck we supposed to do now Iss? We out here in another state and you're going crazy over a bitch that you don't even know. That shit was stupid."

"Yup." Honey looked at me, agreeing with Ziyah before rolling her eyes at Pressure and looking out the window.

"It's not our fault this bitch came out here and couldn't take care of herself. Where the fuck we dropping her at?" Ziyah spoke again. I looked down at Pressure then up at Ziyah before I spoke.

"With us," I told her and when she looked in the rearview mirror at me, I gave her a serious expression.

"You can't be serious?" she asked me, rolling her eyes.

"When have you ever known me to play about some shit like this. While you talking, this could've easily been your dumb ass, or do you not remember that?" I asked Ziyah, looking down at Pressure wondering what the hell she had gotten herself into.

6
TRIGGER (TRIG)

When muthafuckas say it's no place like home, I was feeling that shit right now. Miami was cool but there was nothing like being in the land. Chicago was a dangerous place to live but it was one of the best places to be at the same time. There was nothing like being in my own hood kicking it with my niggas knowing that no matter what happened, muthafuckas would never cross the line where I stayed. When you came to Death Row it was the safest place to be if you were a friend and the worse place to get caught if you were an enemy. We had this area more secure than Fort Knox and niggas knew not to try us.

Every person that we fucked with was like family to us and we all protected the family. You were either going to wear your stripes proud or have a talk with us about it later. I strolled through my back yard making sure everything was in place and putting my weapons of choice in the right spots. When I said this was the safest place in the hood, I wasn't lying muthafuckas could run up if they wanted to, it was definitely going to be a war that they couldn't win. The back of my house and the alley where I stayed was a setup waiting to happen; niggas in the hood didn't don me with the name Trigger for nothing.

When I spoke, they listened, when I said do something, they did that it, because everyone knew I was quick to pull the trigger; fuck the questions and answers after that. I wasn't the type of man to throw my weight around and I didn't bully people, I just wasn't for anyone's bullshit. Most people thought I was crazy, and others got scared at the sight of me. It wasn't because I was a big ass ugly nigga either, most people said I just had that don't fuck with me persona.

"Aye you ready?" I yelled through the house as soon as I hit the back door. I know we had just made it home, but it was business first rest later in this game.

"Here I come nigga." Honey replied irritated. I sat on the couch knowing it was about to take her at least another thirty minutes before she came out the room. I turned on the T.V. to kick back until she was ready. When I heard her heels clicking on the floor as she walked up the hallway, I looked up at her. She swayed her hips as she walked over to me bending over kissing me on the lips. I let my eyes roam over her when she stood back up watching the black trench coat, she had on barely cover her ass. I rubbed my hand over her honey-colored thigh and knew the mark that we were after was going to be all over her tonight.

"I'm ready," she told me in a sexy ass voice that made me want to take her down. My dick jumped, but I had to get myself under control. She knew what it was, and she did that shit on purpose, her light bright eyes got just a little darker as she stared at me. I knew what she wanted; I always knew since the first day I met her crazy ass. I stood up in front of her causing her to take a step back. I gave her a small smile and popped her hard on her ass.

"Let's go," I told her grabbing the keys off the table and walking out the door.

I sat in the back of the bar watching Honey work this nigga over, I knew by the end of the night she would have everything she needed from him, and we could end this. These niggas out her was mesmerized by her and it wasn't only because of her curves and pretty face. Honey had a way with men and this nigga Low was no exception. She had a way of seducing men and women; her game was just that tight. The bitch was literally walking sex appeal with a mind to match it and a slick ass mouth. She could get anything she wanted out of muthafuckas in a short amount of time, and I loved that about her. What people didn't know was she was just as ruthless as I was and that was why we clicked so well.

We only trusted each other and Israel and that was because that nigga was my brother from another mother. Honey came into this game with me seven years ago, the first day we met it was because we were about to rob the same nigga.

I sat in my car and watched her rob this nigga in broad daylight not giving a fuck. I smiled when I saw the look of death in her eyes as she put the gun in the nigga's back. She was in rare form as she went through that nigga's pockets taking everything, he had including his car keys. The man begged for his life once she had everything, she needed from him. Since she took all his shit all I had to do was come along and finish the job or so I thought.

Honey smirked as the man begged for his life, her eyes went cold, and she pulled the trigger without blinking one of her long ass lashes. I bit down on my lip because I knew she was the woman for me, and I was going to get her. Even if I had to toss her thick ass in my trunk and hold her hostage until she had Stockholm's syndrome. Honey walked away from the dead body tucking her gun like nothing had happened. I got out of my car and walked over to her, stepping in front of her. She went for her gun, and I grabbed both of her hands looking down at her.

"I ain't here for that Ma, I'm here for her." I diverted my eyes down to her pussy letting her know what I wanted.

"You on some rapist type shit?" she asked with her face frowned, I laughed a little.

"Naw ma," I let her hands go and stepped back a little.

"You reach for it I'm a slump your ass like you did buddy. As a matter of fact, let's move around; it's about to get hot over here," I told her letting her walk in front of me. She was sexy as hell but if she was anything like me, I'd have a bullet in my head in no time. When she turned to look at me, I nodded my head towards my car for her to get in. Every step she took was with confidence, she looked so sweet and innocent. She didn't seem like the type to do the shit she had just done. She turned and looked at me, stopping at the car, and I shook my head at her.

"You can sit up front with me and act like you got some sense or you can ride in the trunk. The choice is yours." She smiled at me a little and got in the front seat, I pulled my gun out from my waist before getting in the car. I didn't trust her, and she didn't trust me, but after chilling with me for a while she would realize that we were one and the same. I couldn't pass up on a bitch like her because if I did, she would be trying to do the same shit to me that she did to that nigga.

I sat in the car next to her with my gun on my left leg keeping my eyes on the road but on her at the same time until I pulled up on Death Row. She could try that shit she pulled earlier if she wanted to, but she wouldn't make it three steps before she went down. I got out the car and gave her a head nodded to follow me and she complied. Here I could turn my back on her because I knew that my people were watching. Any sudden moves out of her and we would be calling our people to pick her body up. Once we were sitting in my backyard, she put her hands in the air before reaching for her gun and handing it to me.

"What's your name?" I finally asked and waited for her to respond.

"Honey," she replied after what felt like hours. I smirked at her because I knew it wasn't shit sweet about baby girl.

I came out of my thoughts and put my attention back on Honey. I watched her hands as she moved them up Low thigh and knew it was close to the time that we move around. I dropped three-hundred-dollar bills on the table and walked out of the bar. I waited in the car for them to walk out and when they pulled off,

I followed right behind them. Tonight was going to be easy just like any other night like this. This would be pulled off with perfection, get the competition's attention, make them feel comfortable, then take their ass out the game. It was all a part of a plan to keep the family on top and no matter what our family would eat.

7
HONEY

I stood over Low laughing after I had tied him down to the bed, the fear in his eyes was comical. It amazed me how niggas swore they were the toughest muthafuckas around until you put a little pussy in their face. The reality of it was there were only a few real niggas out here in these streets, the rest of them were pons trying to turn themselves into kings. I shook my head at Low when tears started rolling down his face. It never failed, when they knew shit was about to get ugly for them, they cried, and they begged. Shit like that didn't move me though I was as heartless as they come. I took niggas like him out and never batted a fucking eyelash, men like him were weak and weak men didn't need to be alive. I knew I would get everything I had come here for and more because he was crying for his mama.

"I'll double whatever a muthafucka giving you to do this for me. Please don't kill me." Those were the magic words that was like music to my ears. I turned to him, smiling like I was ready to make the deal of a lifetime.

"Okay," I told him, sitting on the bed next to him.

"Give me the code to the safe after I have what I need I'll leave the house and you won't see me anymore." I stared him in his eyes like he could trust me with his life. When I saw relief in his eyes and him exhale a deep breath, I knew it was going to only get easier from here. The only thing that Low should be trusting from me is that I would be taking his life before leaving his house. He ran the code down to me and when I opened his safe, I shook my head. It never failed, their entire life savings in one spot. All the coke he probably owned plus about eighty grand in cash. I pulled out the duffle bag that I had folded up in my big tote bag and stuffed everything in it.

"This isn't double what I was getting," I told him trying to make sure he wasn't hiding anything else. When I saw his chest deflate, I knew it was all he had, and he was trying to think of a way to get me what I needed. I wasted no time signaling Trig to finish him off. One clean shot to the head through the window. I picked up the bag and everything I had come there with and walked out of the house.

"You good?" Trig asked me as soon as I got in the car. It was something that he had done each time after our first hit together. I nodded my head at him before responding.

"Yeah." Trig was so hardcore and I felt like it was his way of softening for me. He knew I was good I had been doing this for a long time, but him asking that made me love him just a little more each time. People never understood how a woman and man that they considered heartless could find love and especially in each other. It was because we were each other in male and female version if that made any sense. Our shit just didn't happen like they do in books. We had to work hard to get to where we are now. It was our interest in the same things that brought us together. Doing shit like this was like a sport to us. At one point we had a competition of who could take down the most opps. Trig made life fun for me; he helped me learn how to trust people again. well, the few people that I did trust.

My life hadn't been easy until I met him, and it didn't surprise me that a man like him could be the one that snatched my soul. I was a rough ass female, and it took a certain caliber of man to grab my attention and get the respect that he deserved from me. Trig snatched me up and demanded respect from the beginning. I knew I was going to be with him the first day we met, and he told me I had two choices. To ride in the front with him or get trunked by him. That crazy shit turned me on, and I knew we was going to be good together.

"Take me to the house, you and Iss handle the count," I told him wanting to go home. He nodded his head and headed towards the house.

I walked up the walkway with my eyes half-closed ready to lay down. As soon as my foot was over the threshold I went straight to the shower. I counted up the days knowing that the day I dreaded was closer than I wanted it to be. My heart sunk as I thought about how my father had died at the hands of the nigga that Trig had saw me kill. Yeah, I pulled off the hit in broad daylight, I hadn't given a fuck about my life. That nigga had taken away the only man that I had loved. That day I didn't give a fuck about going to jail or having the next muthafucka kill me because I had killed him.

My dad was my heart and though he raised me to be a killer just like him, he made sure I had a feminine touch about me. It had just been me and him while I was growing up, I wasn't sure who my mother was or if she was still alive. Knowing my dad, if my mother had decided to cross him in any way, he killed her. I didn't feel anything when it came to a woman that I had never met before, and I don't feel like I missed out on anything by not having a woman around. Shit, John Douglass did a great job raising me in my eyes. He taught me about niggas, and he taught me the best trade a bitch could have.

I learned how to get over on men and women watching him game women and getting them to roll over on their nigga to make sure me and him ate. As I got older, and I felt like I had learned everything I needed from him, I told him six words.

"Put me in the game coach." He did and I have mastered it since then.

I got out of the shower when I heard someone laying on my damn doorbell, it was too late at night for this. All I wanted to do was go to sleep and forget about the fact that I was about to head into a deep depression. I wrapped a towel around me and wiped my feet off on the rug in the bathroom so I wouldn't slip through the house. I ran to the front door and pulled the gun from under the table holding it at my side before opening the door. When I cracked the door to look out no one was there. I looked both ways up the block before looking down to the doorstep. A dozen black roses in a glass vase sat there and caused a chill to go down my spine. I bit down on my lip stepping out the door a little further to pick them up.

I looked around again checking my surroundings before closing the door. My hands shook as I pulled the card out and looked at the handwritten message.

I haven't forgot. I dropped the card and the vase, and it felt like everything was going in slow motion. I had done so much shit along the way that I had no idea who was after me, but I knew it had something to do with my dad because these black roses was his calling card. Someone had taken his signature move of you living out your last days and pulled it on me.

My mouth opened and closed as I tried to think back to the days that I was running with my dad. As soon as he died, I had let the black roses die with him. I liked the element of surprise, and I didn't want you to know I was coming for you. I wanted to see the fear in your eyes when you figured out there was nothing you could do to stop me from getting at you. My father, on the other hand, wanted you to live in fear of not knowing when he was coming for you. So, he dropped a black rose on your car, or in the door of your house, maybe on your kitchen counter or your bed.

I walked off leaving the glass and the roses in the middle of the floor for right now. I was numb and trying to think of who would do this to me. Most people knew who I fucked with, so they never came for me. Besides my dad's old buddies that were still alive, no one knew I was the daughter of the man they called X. This situation right here had me shook as I thought hard about what was going on. I tried to think of every hit me and my dad had done together and came up with nothing. I walked and grabbed everything I needed to clean up this mess before Trig got home. I had to figure out what was going on around me before shit got ugly. The last thing I wanted was to drag my people into some shit they had nothing to do with. They were family and yeah were supposed to protect each other but this had nothing to do with them. This was something that went on before I met them, and I needed to handle it on my own.

I felt another chill go through my body and I knew whatever was happening was going to cost me more than I was willing to give. I had to fix the situation expeditiously and the only thing I continued to come up with was that this had nothing to do with me and it was all about John X Douglass.

8

RILEY

"It's been three days Is and this girl hasn't woke up yet; what the hell you gone do?" I heard an unknown voice of a man ask. I stirred in my sleep, but I wasn't sure where I was at or who I was with. The last thing I remembered was dancing in the club with Jose. Feeling carefree and having the time of my life.

"I told you we should've left that bitch where she was at." A girl stated. My eyes popped open at the venom in her voice. I looked around the room and nothing in here looked familiar. I slowly sat up in the bed, trying to lay my eyes on anything that I could use as a weapon if I needed to. There was nothing remotely close to using and I was beginning to wonder if it was this way on purpose.

"Why the fuck are you even here, Ziyah?" Another male voice said that I thought I knew. I remembered the name being said before and had to think pass the fog that clouded my brain to try and remember something before one of them came in this room.

"Iss you barely let me in your house and I'm your..." her words stopped before she could finish.

Ziyah... Ziyah... I repeated the name in my head and thought back to the day in the store when I looking for something to wear out. Ziyah was the rude ass girl name. Flashes of Miami started to pop up in my head and I started to remember little things from the night at the club. Dancing with Jose, Iss popping up from nowhere, being picked up, and Jose getting knocked out then nothing. I looked down at my clothes and I had on a T-shirt that dropped at my hips with no panties on.

"Exactly, why are you here now?" Iss responded then I heard heels clicking across the floor and a door close. I opened and closed my mouth. It was like sandpaper and all I wanted was some water and my clothes so I could leave. I pushed myself up feeling like I had gotten one of the best sleeps I had ever had in my life. Once my feet hit the floor, the talking stopped and the door open. I stood there in a shirt that barely covered me, staring at Iss and a darker man with an expression that damn near made me piss on myself. I had no idea what to say to them and didn't know if they were about to hurt me. When Iss exhaled a breath, I felt a little relieved, but it didn't stop me from pulling at the bottom of my shirt trying to cover my thick ass thighs.

I knew enough to know that we were not in Miami anymore, and the old self-conscious me came rushing back.

"You had me scared for a minute, Pressure," Iss said, pushing the man that was next to him behind him and closing the door. I crossed my legs back and forth, bouncing from one foot to the other, trying to keep from pissing all over this man's floor.

"I need a bathroom," I told him and he pointed to the corner.

I stood in the mirror looking at myself. I was beat, and I couldn't believe I had been so dumb to not know exactly what had happened to me. I did the best I could to pull myself together in a matter of minutes, but it was very little I could do. I took some deep breaths and walked back into the room with the man that made every part of me tingle. I bit down on my bottom lip before going back out, seeing him sitting on the bed.

He seemed so different from the man I saw going the fuck off on the woman in the store. I left that day because it seemed like he was two different people.

"How did I end up here with you and where exactly is here?" I asked. He shook his head at me, raising both of his eyebrows.

"You got drugged, I stopped you from being raped or whatever else dude had in mind for you, and I brought you back to Chicago." I nodded my head.

"Thank you!" I told him, meaning it, but he just stared at me, picking up a bottle of liquor I never knew he had and putting it to his mouth.

"Aye what the hell was you thinking doing all that shit the other day. You a female out in Miami by yourself and you chose to go out with a muthafucka you barely know than me?" he asked me like I knew who the fuck he was. We had only met twice and to be honest, the same thing could have happened with him. I was kind of stupid to trust a man that I didn't know, but shit, who didn't try to have a one nightstand once in their life?

"I wasn't thinking, I have been through a lot of shit and I just wanted to have fun. Miami seemed like the place I could do that, but I refuse to stand here and be reprimanded by you. Can I have my clothes so I can go Iss?" I asked him. He cocked his head at me like I had lost my mind and the look in his eyes made me take a step back, guarding myself because I had no idea what he was about to do to me. His face was expressionless, but his eyes told me to pipe the fuck down.

"My name is Israel; only my friends and family call me that." He told me and I nodded my head. This nigga must have had a split personality or something because it was almost like he turned into someone else.

"Hey Israel, I'm Riley."

"I know who you are." He told me, cutting me off.

"Listen Pressure, you been out for while... how about we eat some food, and we start all this shit over?" He had gone back to his regular self. I wanted to tell him no but could I really after all he had done for me? This man didn't know me, and he could've tossed my ass in a hospital leaving me in Miami. If nothing else, he deserved for me to at least have dinner or lunch with him.

"Okay but can I shower first?" He nodded his head at me, giving me everything I needed for a shower except clothes. He handed me another T-shirt to put on and from the looks of it, it was just as long as the one I had on. Israel looked me over. I felt a shiver go down my spine. I had to walk away from him, or I would be all over him.

As I showered my mind was racing. I was in the house with the man that made me feel a way I had never felt before just by looking at me. The fact that he had taken care of me and didn't really know me made me feel that much stronger about him. I was happy, I was grateful, and most of all I was horny. I let my hands glide over my body, imagining that they were his. I closed my eyes and let the images of him doing all types of things to me run through my mind. My hands had a mind of their own as they went between my legs to my clit. My mouth opened slightly as I came closer to coming.

I was so into what I was doing I hadn't noticed that the shower door had opened until I felt his mouth on my nipples and his hands replacing mines. My eyes popped open, and I stared at him for minute. His hands never stopped moving and his mouth stayed on me, but his eyes asked for permission. They damn near demanded that I give the okay for him to keep going, I nodded my head. Israel readjusted himself in the shower with me, his mouth never left my body as he dropped his basketball shorts. His dick sprung free and slapped against my skin, making the spot it touched tingle.

His hands slid up my back and he placed his lips on mines shocking me. He lifted me up under my ass picking me up and sliding me onto his dick. His lips never left mines until he was fully inside of me. His eyes popped open, and he pulled back staring at me as I inhaled a breath from the tight fit of him inside of me. He paused for a minute letting me adjust to his length and girth. It felt like Israel had put his dick inside of my stomach and I needed more than a few seconds to catch my breath. I hadn't been fucked in so long that I couldn't even remember how to take the dick anymore.

It was like he knew I hadn't been touched in a while because he held me in place until I nodded my head for him to keep going. He repositioned me placing my legs over his arms and lifted me bringing me down onto him slowly. Low moans started to come from me and got louder as he increased his speed. He put me down on my feet spinning me around facing the tile. I bent over placing my hands on the cold tiles and with one swift move, he was back inside of me.

I bit down on my bottom lip as he placed his hands on my hips and slammed into me. I tried to hold in the sounds of my moans but with each smack to my ass, I couldn't help the sounds that left my mouth. Eventually I gave up, every stroke he delivered hit a spot in me that made me come. I had never had the dick like he was giving it to me; he wasn't selfish, he made sure I was enjoying this just as much as he was. It was when he licked up my spine that made the flood gates open like never before. My body tense, then shook, as I felt the need to pee.

"Come on daddy's dick." His deep voice cut through the fog that was in my head and I did exactly as he demand. I came hard and long I felt my juices leave my body as he grunted increasing his speed. Until his release mixed with mines as I came again. I dropped down because at this point my legs wasn't working. He picked me up then cut the water off stepping out of the shower and dropped a towel over my body. When he laid me on the bed my eyes began to instantly close. I had not a care in the world as I dozed off thinking about how this man I barely knew dicked me down and relaxed me more than I had been in ten years. Again, the words that I heard in the store repeated themselves in my head. *You're safe.*

9

ISRAEL

I watched Riley sleep for a minute before I got up pacing the floor trying to figure out what the fuck was I thinking going in her raw. Not only did I go in her raw not knowing shit about her, but her pussy was so good I couldn't pull out if I wanted to. I had fucked up and I was breaking my own rules once again. When it came to this girl for some reason I couldn't hold back, but I had to be careful with her. I had too much going on in my world to bring a female in that couldn't handle who I was. I was who I was and at my young age, I was set in my ways. I wasn't willing to bend for anyone, not even for a fat ass and some good pussy.

I turned back to her staring at her frame as she slept from the dick, I put on her and wondered why her. I walked over her laying in the bed snoring softly and she looked so peaceful. She seemed totally different from the woman I had met in the store that was timid and ready to run away from me. When I heard a knock at the door, I knew it was the food I had ordered for us. Baby girl had slept for days and after the dick I put on her, I knew she would need some type of nourishment.

I walked to the door and grabbed everything I had ordered because I wasn't sure of what she ate so I ordered some of everything. I grabbed some plates and set everything up on the table feeling like a lame ass nigga. When I walked back in the room and seen her on her side sucking on her bottom lip. I didn't want to wake her up, but she needed to eat. I would hate to see all that thickness waste away. I sat next to her on the bed and lightly shook her until her eyes popped open.

"Yo ass sound like a bear in the forest," I told her as soon as her eyes popped open. She rolled her eyes, mumbled something, and turned her back to me.

"Naw Pressure get up, let me feed you," I told her and when she didn't respond, I grabbed her, standing her on her feet. I wasn't used to people doing shit I didn't tell them, and she was about to learn that the hard way. In a way I felt like I had king's syndrome, I had built up so much, and I had earned my way to have the life that I had. When I spoke muthafuckas listened and it didn't matter who it was, and she was about to have to fall in line if she wanted to fuck with me.

"No, I just want to sleep." She told me laying back on the bed. I nodded my head remembering that she had just woke up from being drugged and not only that I gave her that dope dick. I picked her up and she automatically wrapped her arms around my neck, and I shook my head. In a short amount of time, she had softened my ass and I was going to hate when she had to find out who I was and what I was capable of.

"Come on baby, wake up; time to eat something." I sat her in the chair at the table and her eyes finally popped open to the sight of all the food I had set up. I had gotten steak, seafood, chicken, grilled turkey, baked potatoes, asparagus, and salad. Out of all the shit I had, she was bound to eat something on this table. Her eyes fully popped open when she realized what was sitting in front of her and her stomach growled so loud, I laughed a little.

My phone rung and I knew it was business but for the first time I didn't want to answer it. I knew it was the money but at this time, Pressure had my attention, and I didn't want to focus on anything but her. I felt like a soft ass nigga because I was falling for the same shit, I had told my people never fall for.

"Who supposed to eat all this? I know I got some weight on me but damn." Her eyes were big as she took in everything that was on the table. I smiled a little before dragging my finger across my phone screen to answer it. I nodded my head towards the food for her to eat while I took care of my people on the line.

I walked into my office just listening to what Draco had to say, I picked up my 9millimeter off the desk. As he spoke the angrier I got, I dropped the magazine, pulled back on it taking the bullet out of the chamber, and pointed at the target on the back of the door. I pulled the trigger, imagining that the nigga he was telling me about was at the other end of it.

"How the fuck y'all let this nigga get caught up with fifty grand of work and money?" I asked him, wishing he was on the other end of this gun now as he gave me excuse after excuse. I tried not to be heartless to muthafuckas but that was a lot of money that I had to eat. Now Draco was on the line explaining to me how this nigga Grand got out of jail the same day he got hit. My mind was working overtime trying to figure out how they got to him anyway. His spot was so lowkey that someone had to tell them people that my work was there. I took the gun and scratched the side of my head with it, trying to think of a way to deal with this. Someone on my team of six was talking. For the last few days, I had been in this house playing doctor to a bitch I didn't know, and someone was out here playing with my money.

"All I know is that I saw him walking into his house and when I went in to handle his ass he was gone," Draco replied, and I nodded my head like he was standing in front of me. I hung up the phone without responding to Draco, I was going to personally handle this shit with Grand myself. I had set back and let my team of killers handle my business for so long that muthafuckas in these streets forgot that I was a real chi-town stepper. I hated for people to feel like they could play with me, what I hated more than that was a liar, a thief, and a snitch. Someone was breaking every code that we had put in place for our own safety and protection. It was fucked up, but I had to face the fact that someone in my circle was opening their mouths about shit that was feeding everyone.

I pointed at the target on the door one last time aiming before I put the magazine back in the gun and got up to leave.

I walked out of my house and was in the streets before I realized I had left Riley in my house. I was so concerned about what was going on out here that I didn't think about the fact that she was literally a stranger in my home. I parked my car and pulled up the cameras that I had placed in my home to see what she was doing. Women were naturally curious, and it wouldn't surprise me if she was in my house going through my shit trying to figure out who I was. There really wasn't anything in there but I didn't know her.

I flipped through each room looking for Riley, trying to see what she was up to until I landed on the kitchen. She was putting up the food I had ordered and stacking the dishwasher. I sent out a text to get some information on her as soon as possible. I needed to know who I was dealing with; baby girl seemed cool as hell, and I wanted to fuck with her. She didn't seem like she was cut out for the life I was living though. I put my phone down once she went to the living room and sat on the couch looking down at her phone.

I sat back sipping from my bottle in deep thought trying to figure out, where I went wrong with my people. I took in my surroundings because I wasn't in the right spot to be in my head. As much as I wanted to make Grand a dead issue tonight, I knew it would take more time to get at him. I was a patient man though and I knew everyone would show their hand sooner or later. Right now, I had to get back to the woman that I had left in my house. I wasn't the type of nigga to trust muthafuckas I had known my entire life so to put my trust in her was a non fucking factor. I turned my phone back to the cameras and she was still in the same spot she had sat in on the couch an hour ago. I smiled because she couldn't be this damn sweet, something was up with her. I just had to find out what it was.

Hopefully, it wasn't too much of nothing because if so, I wasn't above making her a memory either.

"Where you need me to drop you off at?" I asked Pressure. She jumped at my words because she had no idea I had been standing there watching her for these last couple of minutes. I shook my head because fucking with a nigga like me she needed to always be alert. I understood why she ended up a target in Miami. It was almost like baby girl had no sense of being in the streets. This only further let me know that she didn't need to be anywhere around me. As much as I liked her and fucking her, she was a liability that I couldn't afford to have at this time. Everyone around me needed to be on point and I didn't have time to teach a baby how to crawl then walk.

"Um, you can just take me downtown to a hotel, I'll be good." I raised an eyebrow at her trying to figure out how the fuck was she partying in Miami but was going to a hotel? I knew I was tipsy, but I wasn't that damn drunk to be stupid. *Who the fuck is this woman?* I questioned myself then walked over to the couch sitting on the coffee table in front of her. As I looked her in her eyes, I felt the person that I tried to keep hidden from her surfacing inside of me. People around me knew it was two sides to me, the person that I liked to show people and the person that came out only when necessary.

"Who the fuck are you?" I cocked my head at her and asked. From the way her eyes went big at the harshness of my question I knew she hadn't expected it.

"I'm... not sure what you mean by that?" she stuttered. I knew it was more from fear than anything. She didn't know me and had no idea of who I was and what I was capable of. I took a deep breath so I could come at this from a different angle.

"Are you the feds?" I asked her.

"Are you fucking crazy?" she asked me. I smirked at her.

"A little," I responded and she got off the couch, quickly trying to walk to the door. I grabbed her by her arm, snatching her to me.

"Answer my question." I demanded through my teeth.

"I thought my question answered yours. No I'm not the fucking feds or the police." She responded with her eyes narrowed at me. I nodded my head at her and pointed at the couch for her to sit back down. She stepped away from me when I let her go but didn't sit down. I knew she was being guarded and appreciated the fact that she had that much sense. She walked back over to the couch but stood behind it instead of sitting down. I watched her and the way she moved; her demeanor had changed.

"Why are you going to a hotel instead of home?" I asked her. It took her a while to collect her thoughts, like she was trying to figure out how much information she wanted to give me. She stared me in my eyes for a long time before she came back to sit on the couch.

"I came from a bad situation. Before I left for Miami, I sold my house and honestly the only place I have to go is a hotel." I nodded my head at her words and was about to respond when a text came to my phone. The text had no name and only five numbers at the top and I knew it was the information I had asked for earlier.

CURTIS'S WIFE, HE'S NOT DEAD.

I never let my expression change as I read the words in all caps. My heart sunk because it was ten years later, I hadn't heard anything about him until now. This nigga had sent his wife in to take care of some shit that he wasn't man enough to take care of.

"What do you mean a bad situation?" I continued to probe to see all of what she would tell me. She told me about how she

six that sat at the table were all looking at each other
y were enemies. I knew I couldn't ask for help when the
asn't trusting each other. All of this shit was just bad
and I felt like we were all being attacked from different
I couldn't add anything else to an already full plate and
was going through would tip the scale because Trig and
ld do what was necessary to protect the family. Like I
o what was necessary if they were in this predicament.
t into my car placing my gun on my thigh and starting it
ld get home. I had never been a scary type of person and
w who was behind this I wouldn't be scared now. There
many unknown components in this situation that I was
ng to question if my team was going through all of this
of me. I questioned everything I seen and didn't see and
thing I wanted was for one of them to get hurt behind
it that was going on with me.
ile I was at the light, I took a couple of breaths to get
together, because if I was stressing, I knew I couldn't be
t. I checked my mirrors to make sure I wasn't being
d and took off as soon as the light turned green. My
rung and my evil twin popped up on the screen with a
ext to it and I smiled. I hit the button in my steering
o answer the phone and I felt my entire world tilt.

❧

r I'm a kill whoever the fuck was behind this." I heard
then I blacked out.
h, she's going to come through this she's a fighter." Iss
n then I blacked out again.
u're the only bitch I can trust, you have to make it
this." Ziyah whispered then I blacked out again.
ddy?" I questioned knowing this man was dead. I couldn't
g him unless I was dead too.
u're doing good Honey keep your eyes open for me." A

was married young, and things didn't go like she thought it would. Told me after dealing with not being loved for so long she finally decided that it was time to take her life back. I would have felt sorry for her, I hated to hear about women being abused by men, but she was the wife of the enemy. Everything that came out of her mouth I felt was a lie. I didn't show her that I felt her words was bullshit. I took in everything that she was telling me and made her think I could be her listening ear.

"I hate to hear you went through that; it's fucked up that a man you gave your heart to would fuck you over like that." I watched her facial expression as the words left my mouth. This bitch was good at pretending and it only made me angrier that she could sit in front of me and lie with a straight face. I had saved her fucking life and she was over here feeding me bullshit.

"It's cool, it was an experience that made me figure out what I don't want out of life." *Damn, she's smooth,* I thought to myself. I listened to her talk for a little while longer and thought about that old saying. Keep your friends close and your enemies closer.

"Listen Pressure, the more you sit here and talk I can tell that you have missed out on a lot. I'm willing to make you a proposition that I think can benefit both of us."

"What's that?" she asked. Seeing the curiosity on her face I knew that no matter what I was about to say she would be willing to go with it. Baby girl was looking for excitement in her life and she was going to get more than she bargained for fucking with a nigga like me. I smiled a little before I spoke.

"Let's ride the wave together." She raised her eyebrow trying to figure out what I was getting at.

"Meaning?" she questioned.

"Let's fuck around, no commitment, no rules, we do what we want to do, when, where, and how we want to do it. You can stay here with me for the time being if you want to and when we both decide it's over, that's what it is." She looked at me skeptically, like she didn't like what I had come up with. If I don't know anything else, I knew that I could convince a muthafucka to do what I wanted them to do, and she wasn't any different. If she didn't go for it now, she would go for it later, like I said I was a patient man.

As she sat in front of me thinking about what she wanted to do, I knew I had her right where I wanted her when she looked me in the eyes biting down on her lip.

"We don't even know each other." She stated.

"How can we get to know each other if we don't put in time to? I know this shit is out the blue, but you know I wouldn't do anything to hurt you. I think I proved that when I got you safely back to Chicago," I told her, laying it on thick. For this to work in my favor I needed her to trust me completely, and it wasn't anything I wouldn't say or do to get the results that I wanted. When all this shit was over, Curtis and her would be resting peacefully as husband and wife.

"Okay." I smiled when the word left her mouth, and I knew I would have to put in work to get her exactly where I wanted her.

10

HONEY

I tried my best to stay calm as I
single black rose stuck in the wi
my purse, gripping my nine as I l
if someone was watching me. A few
failed that once a week these roses wo
all my father's old associates just to fee
one of them were up to it. None of the
too old school, and their loyalty went b

It was to the point that I had beco
of the house by myself. Don't get me w
shit at the drop of a dime, but I was no
case the predator had turned into the
out how my life changed so drastically
time. I still hadn't let Trig or the others
They had other things to worry about
and one of the people that sit at th
against the fold. They knew it was
because no one knew about Grand b
their best kept secrets, but with him f
tion, we knew it was only a matter of t
and killed.

The
like the
team w
timing
angles.
what I
Iss wo
would
I g
so I co
if I kn
were s
beginn
becaus
the las
some s
Wh
myself
on poi
followe
phone
heart
wheel

"I swe
Trig sa
"Br
told hi
"Yo
throug
"D
be seei
"Yo

voice that wasn't my father's said as I blinked several times so my eyes could adjust to the light they were putting in my eyes.

"Daddy!" I said again a little louder and Trig's head popped over the doctor's shoulders.

"I'm here baby it's going to be okay. I got to you as soon as I could." I let my eyes fall on everything around me before I realized that I was being rushed through the hospital. Paramedics and doctors surrounded me talking fast and ripping my clothes off of me.

"What happened to me?" I asked as people rushed me into a room moving me from the stretcher to the bed in the emergency room.

"You were involved in a hit and run; you took a bad hit. You were in and out of consciousness on the scene and we have to make sure you are okay." One of the doctors told me and I thought back to what I was doing before I couldn't remember. Flashes came to me of answering the phone while driving down the street. I smiled as soon as I was about to say hey then I was hit by a big ass black truck. My truck flipped over and the infamous black rose fell to the ground right before I blacked out. I begin to fight, trying to hit everyone in front of me, I couldn't trust anyone around me.

"Ma'am you have to calm down." One of the people around me said as I fought my hardest to get up out of the bed. I could care less what they wanted to do and how they wanted to try and help me. The best thing for me to do was to get out of here, the hospital was one of the worse places to be at a time like this.

"Trig! Trigger!" I called out his name because I know he would listen to me, he would save me, even if no one else tried. I needed him close, I needed him to keep eyes on everyone around me. For the first time in my life, I felt that I needed to be saved, I wanted to feel protected by the man that I had given my all to.

Trig busted through the door with a gun in both of his hands trained on the nurses and doctors in the room. I would have smiled at my thug and shining armor if pain wasn't slicing through my head and body.

"What the fuck are y'all doing to her?" He asked through his teeth. His eyes cut to me then back at the doctors and nurses. He was ready to shoot anyone of them at the drop of a dime over me. I loved him for being the protector that I always knew he was, he wasn't willing to play about me and Iss damn sure would drop anybody over him. It was so much I wanted to say to him in that moment, but I couldn't. Watching him with guns pointed at everyone over me brought me back to reality. He had no idea what was going on with me. I hadn't enlightened him about anything concerning the roses or my past. Whoever was after me, might end up coming for him if I told him. I didn't want to lose my life, but I couldn't let him lose his either. I had to be the one to protect him from the bullshit that was going on with me. Laying in this room I was mentally weakened. I had let everything I had been taught go right out of my head. *I was built for this shit, I was strong, I am strong.* I told myself as my eyes roamed over Trigs tattooed covered skin. I loved him too much to let this be my last time seeing him, so that mean no matter what happened while I was in here, I had to fight.

"I love you baby!" I told him and he lowered his guns and cocked his head at me.

"Yeah?" he asked with a crooked smile on his face.

"Yeah!" I told him just as Iss was pulling him out of the room. I could hear from his tone he was cursing Trig's ass out, but I couldn't make out what he was saying. I smiled a little before I felt a small prick in my arm, and I dozed off to sleep.

11
TRIG

A month had passed, and Honey was still fucked up over what had happened. Physically she was fine, but she was different. We were grateful that she had only came out of that accident with a concussion because it could've been way worse. Her truck was damn near folded in half and flipped upside down when I had gotten to her. Iss, Ziyah, and me made it to the scene before the police and ambulance, but that wasn't shit new for Chicago. Hell, it had been times that bodies lay on the ground uncovered for hours. It was a damn shame, but the truth is, that's just how it was.

I sat in the chair on the side of the bed in the dark waiting for Honey to wake up. We had to get some things clear around here. I wasn't one of those niggas that saw my girl going downhill and ignored it, then months later wondering why she killed herself. Nope, I paid attention to everything, that was my strength and my weakness because I see shit, I shouldn't see all the time. Just like with Honey, as much as she tried to make it seem like nothing was bothering her, I knew it was. She seemed more paranoid than anything and since she wasn't a weed smoker this was a new trait she was showing.

It made me wonder what could make a woman like her

scared of anything. She was the same woman that killed and robbed a man in broad daylight, the same woman that hit licks with me on daily basis. She was the same woman that wasn't scared to pop her shit if she had to. Honey was my ride or die, my right hand, and my heart so it made me wonder what in the hell was going on that she felt like she couldn't talk to me about. I can admit I'm not the let's sit down and hold hands and talk about your feelings kind of nigga. She knows I fuck with her and if she needs to talk about anything I care enough to listen.

Honey stirred in her sleep, and I felt when her eyes opened and her staring in my direction.

"Why are you being a creep?" she asked me, and I shook my head turning on the bedside lamp.

"What the fuck you keeping secrets for?" I questioned, ready to get everything out of the way. Honey huffed like she didn't want to talk about whatever was on her mind, but I wasn't about to settle for her closing herself off to me. Although she was a cold-hearted killer, the side that she showed the people she loved was another side of her. When it had nothing to do with business Honey was normally a happy person. She loved to be affectionate with me and if she saw a woman that she was into she would be the first to flirt with them.

Before the accident she had changed a little, but now shit had drastically changed. I sat and waited for her to say something. At this point she could just about tell me anything to help me understand what was going on with her. I sat back in my chair stretching my legs in front of me watching her. Honey didn't make any movements that would be tell signs of her lying. When her demeanor changed, I knew she was about to come with the bullshit.

"Before you speak, don't treat me like I'm one of your marks."

"What?" she questioned, staring at me.

"Honey, I know you better than any other muthafucka we are around. I'm the nigga you lay next to every night. I'm the same man that watch you pull that same shit with niggas we about to dead." She nodded her head at me, and her persona changed again.

"My bad baby, I just don't want to seem weak." I searched her eyes, and she was telling the truth.

"You've never been a weak ass bitch Honey; you harder than most niggas I know." She smiled at my words and I knew she was loosening up.

"I'll tell you what, if you tell me what's going on, daddy will give you something nice." She sat up in the bed staring at me. Honey loved new shiny toys and I had come prepared for her spoiled ass.

"I'm just fucked up over the entire hit and run thing." She began to speak, and I sat up to give her my full attention.

"Shit happens baby, you don't have to worry about that. Whoever did that will get handled, that's my word," I told her, meaning what I said, but what was getting me was the expression on her face. It was almost like she was worried, or she was questioning my ability to protect her. When I stared at her, her eyes softened for me, and she smiled a little.

"It's just that I feel like I was slipping when this happened, if I was more alert, I might have been able to react differently. Isiah." She used my real name, I cocked my head at her because I knew she was about to tell me some real shit.

"I know that you would protect me with your life, so don't look at me like that. I'm just in my feelings about this shit, it has nothing to do with you, all of this is personal. I'm still your ride or die, I'm still the bitch that you threatened to put in the trunk when we met. I'm just kicking my own ass right now," she told me honestly.

"I'm not going to disregard your feelings, but shit happens, Honey, and this situation is not on you. It could have happened to any one of us. Now get out your feelings because I got something for you," I told her and she smiled at me.

I pulled the box from under the chair and her eyes lit up like a kid on Christmas day. I handed her the medium sized gift, she looked at me then opened it. When she pulled out the new chrome and blue baby nine-millimeter that was wrapped in the diamond encrusted Cuban link chain she smiled. I wasn't the flowers and candy type of nigga, but I did my thing when it came to her. She got out the bed and jumped in my lap kissing my lips and dropped to her knees. When her lips wrapped around my dick, I couldn't help but to inhale a breath. I grabbed her head and pushed her mouth down further on me until my dick was down her throat. She didn't gag she took all of me like she was a pro. I sat back and enjoyed her topping me off, she kept her mouth wet as she slid her mouth up and down on me. When I felt myself about to bust, I pulled her head up.

"Grab your ankles," I told her and she bent over at my command, her ass spread in front of me. I smacked her on it, and she twerked making her ass jiggle right before I slammed into her. She knew how I was coming. I was giving her long deep strokes watching her juices hit the floor as her body vibrated. I smacked her ass again harder making her cry out, before picking her up putting her on the bed. I got down on my knees in front of her and licked her pussy. I ate her pussy until she was trying to run away from a nigga. I never wanted her to worry about shit, I was here for anything she needed from me.

12

RILEY

I sat at the table in Israel's house not believing what had happened between us in a short amount of time. This man made me feel like I was the only woman in the world. It was totally different from being with Curtis. Iss was thoughtful, smart, attentive, and stimulating in more ways than one. He not only seduced my body, but he seduced my mind, he asked questions and did things to challenge me. In his world, I wasn't the caretaker, I wasn't the maid, I was all woman, and he did everything within his power to show me that I was.

With him I could free fall, with him I could jump off the cliff and know that I would grow wings and fly. He was just that much of a man in my eyes, being with him was doing something to me it was changing me. The nigga had me wrapped around his finger and didn't even know it. I was pass falling, I had fallen hard, and was questioning my sanity about how quick it happened. Is this even real? Did shit like this happen in real life? I asked myself for the hundredth time in a matter of weeks. I was in love, and I knew it was real because it was totally different from the crush that I had on Curtis.

I was eating, sleeping, and breathing Israel and it was because he was one of the realest people I had ever met. In my eyes it was nothing under the sun this man could do that would make me change the way I felt about him. Israel was a smooth ass nigga and I eating up everything he was giving me with a silver spoon. The things he did to my body was something for the books, I had never met a man like him and I questioned if there was another one like him. We said we were riding the wave but what was I going to do when that was over? I knew I could never find another man that could treat me even as close as he did.

All the diamonds, purses, and gifts that he gave me was just an added bonus to the man he was. He didn't give them to me to shut me up or so I could look good in front of his friends, he did it just to see the smile on my face. I had fell for a nigga I barely knew, and it amazed me, but I was waiting for the other shoe to fall.

I knew love was blind, but I wasn't dumb, it was more to him than meets the eye. It would be times we would be out with his friends, and I would see how they were with him. They respected and feared him at the same time. I snapped out of my thoughts when my phone rung, I looked at my screen and smiled when I saw his name there.

"Hey, baby," I told him with a smile on my face.

"Pack us a small bag and meet me at the airport at three; bring your passport and grab mines out of the drawer."

"Okay," I told him, hanging up the phone and heading to the room.

I stopped in my tracks when I heard a knock at the door; no one ever came here unless Israel was here. I took my time walking to the door hoping the person would just leave but they continued to knock. I looked out of the peep hole, and it was Ziyah standing on the other side dressed to kill. I opened the door and she walked past me without saying a word.

"Israel isn't here," I said and she turned to me.

"I know," she replied and stared at me like she was disgusted with me. Her eyes roamed from my feet all the way up to my eyes then she rolled her eyes like I had done something to her. I cocked my head at her, she hadn't liked me since she first laid eyes on me. Personally, I didn't care, I wasn't here for her. Her opinion of me didn't stop shit I had going on and it didn't stop Israel from fucking with me. I didn't give a fuck if she fucked with me, I had learned a long time ago as long as I fucked with myself no one else mattered.

"What can I do for you?" I asked her with a tight smile on my face.

"You can leave Iss alone." She folded her arms over her chest and smacked her lips before she spoke. I stepped back because the bitch had the audacity to come here and make demands over a man that acted like she didn't exist most of the time. I saw the way she looked at him when she thought no one was looking. Baby girl was in love, you could see it every time she was around. She would jump to do what he needed before he opened his mouth to ask for it. I couldn't fault her for how she felt. Israel was a hell of a man when he wasn't being an asshole to her.

"Why would I do that?" I asked her seriously.

"Because you don't belong here, you think you know who he is? You know nothing about him, you couldn't handle the real him if you knew the truth. This shit y'all got going on here is a façade. Bitch if you knew the truth about him you would be running back to the burbs with your fucking tail between your legs." I laughed at her a little.

"Now I'm a dog?" I asked her, shaking my head.

"If he knew what I knew about you, you would be a dead ass dog," Ziyah replied and for the first time since she got here, I was intrigued. I had no idea what she had conjured up in her head about me, but I was sure whatever she thought she had on me wasn't true. I was an open book and why would Israel want to kill me. He wasn't even the person she was making him out to be with that statement. The smirk she wore on her face let me know even further that she felt like she had the key to getting rid of me.

"You don't know me well enough to say that you have that type of information on me," I told her.

"I don't have to know you to get what I need on you. I'm going to tell you one last time to leave, and we can pretend that you were never here," she told me. I put my hands on my hips to show her there was no way in hell I was leaving Israel just because she wanted me to.

"Girl fuck you; you can let yourself out. I have something to do," I told her, walking away from her.

"Curtis," she said his name and I turned towards her wondering what he had to do with anything. She smiled at me like she had just hit the jackpot. I wasn't sure what she meant by this but after her dead dog statement, I was hoping she wasn't saying she would do something to him. Instead of showing her that she had gotten to me I decided to stay stoic.

"What about him, Israel already knows that I was married," I told her, hoping this was what she was referring to.

"It's not that you were married, it's who you married." I raised an eyebrow at her trying to figure out what the fuck she was getting at. Israel and Curtis didn't even run in the same circles. I hadn't asked Israel what he'd done for a living, but he didn't seem like the type to be in the streets.

"What does my ex-husband have to do with this?" Her smile was mischievous as she nodded her head at my question.

"Everything."

I squinted my eyes at her, I felt like she was trying to play games with me.

"Just tell me whatever the fuck you came here to say," I was getting irritated with her presence. I couldn't feed into her bullshit any longer, she was wasting my time with her antics. I had wasted so much time over the last ten years that I wasn't willing to let another second go by with her bullshit. Although she had my attention with some of her words it was time for her ass to talk or walk. I moved past her and opened the door since me telling her to let herself out earlier didn't work. Ziyah had come in here and was fucking up what had started out as a good day. I couldn't give her anymore of my time, that was the one of the things that I held dear to me at this moment in my life. To be honest, she was messing with several things that I was trying to hold on to since I left that mad house, I called a home. All I wanted to do was live my best life, have fun, and find myself while keeping a peace of mind. My previous life was so hard that I wanted everything that came after that to be easy. Ziyah was standing in front of me trying to take all that I wanted away from me.

"You so lost when it comes to Iss that you can't even see what's right in front of you," she told me, shaking her head.

"That nigga's so smooth and he has you thinking that he's someone that he's not. Why he softens himself for you I will never know? I'll tell you what though, I know about this little trip he's taking you on. When y'all get back I advise you to pack your shit and leave because if not you're going to find out who the real nigga is behind that front he puts on for you shorty." Her words were like a smack to the face. I could look at what she was telling me as her being a bitter bitch, but for some reason I didn't. She was right I didn't know Israel, but I felt him.

A chill ran down my spine as she stared at me like she was ready to kill me. I had heard of bitches like her before. Females that did anything to have the man that they loved, they weren't above tossing a bitch in Lake Michigan just to have their way.

I stared back at her with my hand still on the doorknob and my back to the open door. I felt him behind me before I saw the expression on Ziyah's face change. She looked like she had saw a ghost as her face went pale.

"Get the fuck out." He told her through his teeth, both Ziyah and I jumped at his harsh tone. Ziyah cut her eyes at me and tapped her wrist before walking out of the door.

Israel walked in the house and stood in front of me.

"What was that about?" he asked me, staring into my eyes. I wanted to tell him everything that had transpired between Ziyah and me in that short amount of time. For some reason, I couldn't; for the first time since I had been with him, I wanted to withhold information from him. I needed to sit back and think about everything she told me.

"She loves you," I told him a half-truth that I was sure he already knew. I wasn't big on lying to the people that I cared about, and I wasn't about to start now.

"That's it?" his voice was stern like he was daring me to lie to him, like he knew what had been said behind closed doors. I stared him in the eyes because that's how I was able to tell what he was feeling more so than what he was thinking.

"Israel, I have no reason to lie to you. I can say for sure that Ziyah's reason for being here today was because she is in love with you." He stared at me for a few seconds and for the first time since I had been around him my heart began to beat faster from fear. He didn't have to say a word to me, he didn't have to threaten me, but them damn eyes of his said it all. Just as quick as the threat crossed his eyes it left, and he softened for me smiling.

"Let's get ready to go," he told me.

13

RILEY

I sat on the private jet across from Israel watching him sleep. He seemed to be so at peace in the air, most times at night he tossed and turned. He barely had a good night's sleep unless he was drunk as hell, or we were at a hotel. I sat back thinking about the time we had spent together trying to put together the pieces of the puzzle concerning him. I thought about all the drinking, and the nights that he came in the house like his mind wasn't at ease. On those nights, I would hand him something to drink and when he was done, I would rub his body down. I would light some sage and use my special blend of oils to massage his entire body until he was no longer tense. Then I would end it by giving him some head and pussy if he wasn't totally out of it by then.

I was in love, but I wanted to make him feel just as special as he made me feel. Now I was sitting back thinking that me trying to give him what he was giving me made me miss something. I had overlooked the times that things didn't seem right because all I could see was the man that he wanted me to see. He stirred in his sleep a little opening his eyes to look at me then was back out. We had another couple of hours in the air before we landed, and I wanted to clear my head of everything that had happened today. I wanted to use this time to get past the fog in my head about Israel, for some reason I wasn't thinking clearly enough to catch on to what was going on around me.

I bit down on my lip in deep thought staring out of the window looking at the clouds below us.

"What's on your mind?" Israel asked when I turned to him his eyes were still closed.

"I thought you were sleep," I told him looking back out of the window.

"I was for a minute, but you were thinking too loud." I smiled at his words. This was one of the reasons I was hooked on this man. It was damn near like he felt things going on with me in the atmosphere.

"What made you come to the house today after you had told me to meet you?" He finally opened his eyes and sat his seat up staring at me.

"I saw Ziyah was there on the cameras, she knew I wasn't there, I knew she was on some bullshit." I nodded my head at him, the entire time I had been at his home he was watching me.

"Do you watch me in the house a lot?" I asked him and he cocked his head at me.

"Not as much as I used to."

"Why were you watching me anyway?" I asked. I should've felt creeped out by his revelation, but I didn't. I just wanted to understand where he was coming from.

"I have a hard time trusting people." This was the same man that bought me back from Miami and watched over me until I was fine. I trusted him with my life, but he couldn't trust me to be in his home that he asked me to stay in.

"I don't get it Iss, you wanted me there, you trust me enough to go into my body without protection, but not enough to be in your home alone." He nodded his head at me.

"I thought we had an understanding, and you want me to take you for your word, but you won't take me for mines. I would never intentionally do anything to hurt you."

"How can you say that when you have no idea who I am Pressure? You only see to what I allow you see; I would never want you to get a glimpse of who I actually am." His words were like ice water rushing through my veins. Ziyah was right I had no idea who I was fucking with, but what I was feeling for him made me want to find out who he really was. I know we hadn't been around each other for a long time, but it felt like a lifetime. Israel had two different sides to him and could I really love one side without loving and knowing the other side.

"Listen Iss, I fuck with you and I'm fucking with you, you don't have to pretend and put on a show for me. Keep all this shit a buck with me and we can work out the kinks as we go," I was feeling the little bit of hood I had in me coming out. I hated to feel lied to and tricked, I was a grown ass woman and this conversation I was having with him made me feel like I was being handled. I had turned a blind eye to so much stuff over time that all I asked for was complete honesty from him. I gave him the truth willingly and thought he would do the same with me, but I guess I was wrong.

"Riley, I only give you what you need to know about me, it's not about pretending to be someone else. I am who the fuck I am." My eyes got big at how he was talking to me, his tone and everything changed with me, I had struck a nerve. The usually calm man that I had seen daily was gone.

"The person that I am with you is still me Riley, it's just a side of me that I can barely show to others because of everything that I have going on." I cocked my head at him.

"What do you have going on that's so bad that you can't tell me huh?" My attitude was switching up on him and from the look in his eyes, I knew he didn't like it. At this point, I had been completely honest, and I wasn't a small ass child that didn't know how to handle myself. Whatever he was keeping from me was for his protection and not mines. If I was smart, I would have let it go, but I wasn't being smart. I was acting like a woman in love.

"What do you do for a living?" It was time to let the this shit out; I was flying in the clouds, but my head wasn't there anymore. Ziyah had threatened me with bodily harm if I hadn't left him alone. She was basically telling me that him and my ex was enemy's. When it comes to the streets, if Curtis was an enemy of Israel's, then so was I. Although Curtis hadn't been in the streets since he was almost killed, real street beef never died. That meant I was fair game to whatever they had going on even though I had never been for the streets.

"Investments." He replied, staring me straight in my eyes. "I see Ziyah been in your ear about me, what the fuck did she tell you?" His tone changed again making me cut the stare between us.

"She enlightened me," I told him and he moved up in his seat, getting closer to me, grabbing my chin between his index finger and his thumb.

"Listen to me Pressure, I don't want to be the person I know you wouldn't like. Normally you have a way of centering and calming the storm inside of me, but today you trying to take me there. I'm not the type of nigga you want to play with and the shit you're pulling on this jet is the type of attitude I don't tolerate. I'm letting you know now we can keep this shit real cordial, or you can get the side of me you been begging to see these last few minutes." He let my chin go and I made sure to break eye contact with him. I knew when enough was enough and I was pushing him hard. I had to sit back and ask myself if I really wanted to see who this man was, because sometimes when you let the beast out of the cage it was hard to put it back in.

I sat back in my chair and crossed my legs, Israel's eyes stayed on me studying every move I made. I took a deep breath and exhaled it looking him in his eyes, the little bit of anger he showed me actually turned me on and I was ready to drop to my knees in front of him just to get some of this tension I had caused out the air. Sex wasn't going to help what I was about to do though, instead of leaving him like Ziyah suggested I do, it was at this moment I decided to tell him who I was married to. In my eyes this streets didn't matter, Curtis had been out of the game for a long time and after ten years everything about the game had changed. The niggas and females out in the streets didn't care anymore. Anyone was fair game and there was no code of loyalty amongst the people in the streets. After speaking to Ziyah, I knew that Israel wasn't who he was portraying himself to be.

I watched his demeanor and recognized the air that he had about himself now. This nigga was for the streets, exactly how deep that went I didn't know. At this point, I didn't want to know. I just wanted to make it back to Chicago alive. His mannerisms spoke volumes and demanded my respect.

"I think we need to talk about something," I bit down on my lip trying to figure out exactly how I was going to approach the subject. His demeanor changed again he relaxed a little.

"You can tell me anything, you know that." He told me seriously. I contemplated for a minute then just opened my mouth. I had to be ready for whatever was going to come after what I was about to say.

"Remember when we first started talking and I told you I had been married?" he nodded his head giving me the floor waiting for me to continue.

"Well, I never told you who I was married too; it wasn't intentional, I just didn't think it was any of your business. He was my past, and you were a fling." I closed my mouth before I continued while I was babbling, I hadn't thought before I spoke. What if I hurt his feelings calling him just a fling when he had proven to be more than that to me. Israel wasn't a fling to me; he was the nigga that I wanted to wake up to every morning and go to bed with at night. Most people would think it was because of the dope ass pipe that he laid on me every chance he got, but it wasn't. It was him, the man, the smooth ass nigga that had my panties wet at this moment with just the look he was giving me.

14
ISRAEL

I sat back watching Riley as she fidgeted like she was scared to tell me who she was married to. I made a mental note to get in Ziyah's ass for opening her mouth about this. Pressure didn't have to tell me what Ziyah had told her, the audio on the cameras worked well. I would have turned up on her ass when she was at the house, but we had a plane to catch. Due to her unexpected visit, we were running late anyway. What pissed me off more than anything was that if I hadn't figured out that Pressure wasn't trying to get back at me for Curtis, Ziyah would have ruined my plans.

Pressure was a lot of shit when it came to her make up but trying to get back on some street shit was the last thing she was about. She was showing me that she was genuine in the way that she acted and the things that she did. I saw the fear cross her eyes as she was about to open her mouth again.

"I know who you were married to," I told her, taking her out of her misery.

"If you knew, why didn't you tell me that he was an old enemy of yours? Why would you make me comfortable around you? Why would you make me lo...?" She closed her eyes in frustration, taking a deep breath.

"I have my reasons," I told her and she got up from her seat, pacing the floor.

"Did you know when we were in the store? Was Miami a ploy to get back at him?" I cocked my head at her; she did have a reason to ask all of these questions but was I willing to give her the answers. With her being who she was I still couldn't fully trust her, what if she went back and told this nigga everything.

"If I knew who you were in Miami, I would have left you with the Cuban nigga I took you from," I told her the truth and she dropped down in the seat across from me.

"When you found out why did you still fuck with me?" I got up and grabbed a bottle of D'Ussé' from the bar. I wasn't used to being questioned but like I said, Pressure had a right to ask me everything that she was asking. I didn't get a glass to drink out of. I was going to hit this shit straight from the bottle. After I answered her question, she was going to want to hit from this bottle too.

"Because I was going to kill you," I told her, looking her in the eyes then I handed her the bottle. She was going to need something strong to swallow what I had just told her. Not only had I told her my attentions, but I kind of told her the type of man I was. Pressure hit the bottle a couple of times and handed back to me like we were two of the fellas on the block kicking it.

What she didn't realize is that her vibe was amazing, she was so fucking smart, and I had a thing for smart ass women. I fucked with her the long way; at this point I wouldn't do shit to hurt her, I just wanted to protect her from everything bad in the world. It was rare that you found women like her these days, all bitches wanted was money and dick. I was willing to give them the dick and keep it moving, but with Pressure it was something else. She came with her own bag and that just made me want to give her more because she never asked me for anything. The gifts and shit that I gave her she could buy herself, I just wanted to put a smile on her face.

She would be the perfect woman for me if I thought she

could handle everything I was in to, but in my eyes, she couldn't. She wasn't built to go out and grab a package if I needed her too, she would question every move I needed her to make. It was smart on her behalf because it lets me know that a nigga couldn't pull nothing over on her, but I needed a woman that would move with precision when I told them too. Therefore, I kept her hidden and protected from the life I was living. I already had to fight demons from this shit, but it would put a hole in my heart if I had to put a bullet in hers.

"You were going to kill me?" she questioned with tears in her eyes, and it fucked me up because I hated to see a woman cry.

"Hell yeah, no one jeopardizes what I have going on, but that was before I got to know you. That was before I figured out you have nothing to do with anything and our paths crossing was an act of fate. Maybe it was so you could leave that nigga, maybe it was so I could save your thick ass in Miami," I told her honestly.

"And now?" she questioned, and I turned the fifth up, handed it to her, and watched her do the same thing.

"Now I fuck with you," I told her shrugging my shoulders not sure if she would decide to finish what we had going on or leave. In my mind I was saying fuck it if she does, but my heart was hoping she would find a way to push through this shit.

"I know this probably won't mean nothing to you, but I apologize. Before you start rolling your eyes and shit, you should know that I don't apologize to anyone for anything." She turned the bottle up to her beautiful ass lips again. From how low her eyes were, I could tell she was feeling the liquor, which was expected because she wasn't a hard liquor drinker. She stood up putting the bottle under her arm and began clapping.

"Well thank you for not killing me." She rolled her eyes and stumbled back into her seat, wasting part of the liquor on her arm. When she looked down at her arm and began licking it off, I forgot about everything we had been going back and forth about.

"Pressure," I called her name and she looked up at me

sucking on her bottom lip. This fucking woman always got to me; I couldn't control myself with her especially when liquor was involved.

I smirked at her because I knew her pussy was throbbing and ready for me to take that shit. I dropped down to my knees in front of her, pushing up the sun dress she had on and stuck my finger inside of her. I was about to take finger fucking to another level on this plane. She opened her legs wider for me as she moaned. Her juices were covering my fingers, I pulled them out looked her in her eyes and licked one of them. She grabbed my hand. taking the rest of my fingers in her mouth, then chased her own juices with the liquor she was holding. I let her seat back and pulled her ass to the end of it. When I put my head between her thighs, she wrapped her legs around my neck as I took my tongue across her whole pussy. Then I used the tip of my tongue and made circles on and around her clit. She rolled her hips as I placed one hand under her to pull her closer to my mouth. I listened to her moans as they changed with each lick, I gave her. I inserted my index finger back into her finding her g spot and tapped it until her honey was covering my mouth. She let out a scream and tightened her legs around my neck until she was done coming.

"You forgive me?" I asked her as she was trying to catch her breath. When she looked up at me, I knew she had but I wanted to hear the words from her. I pulled my dick out of my pants and she licked her lips I knew what she was on. She sat up in her seat and before I could push her head back, her lips were wrapped around my dick like a vice grip. I closed my eyes and exhaled a breath when she went all the way down on me to my nuts. Pressure was on this jet trying to prove a point and damn near had me moaning like a little bitch. When she went back down on me, the tip of my dick hit the back of her throat she hummed and moved her head from side to side causing my knees to buckle a little.

I pulled from her mouth and smacked her thigh so she could

bend over for me. She did it without me opening my mouth and put the perfect arch in her back. When I went inside of her, I paused for minute, because no matter how many times I fucked her, she had some of the best pussy and head I gotten in my life. When I was all the way in her she moaned, and I smacked her ass.

Pressure was about to take this dick while we were in the air, and I wasn't going to let up until she told me she forgave me. I smacked her hard on her ass right before I gave her the first stroke.

"Say you forgive me," I told her smacking her on the ass. Her ass jiggled upon impact and fucking her right now was like the battle of the sexist, she was pulling out every trick and trade she could. She worked her muscles on me and was continually throwing her ass back on me. I grabbed her by her hair, pulling her head back as far as it could go, slamming into her with no mercy.

"Say it!" I told her. Her eyes closed and sucked on her bottom lip to keep the worlds from leaving her mouth. I wanted to hear the words come from her, I knew all was forgiven when she opened her legs up to me.

"Trust me," she replied and I damn near stopped mid-stroke. The only person I trusted one hundred percent was myself and she was asking me for something that I couldn't give. I had been crossed so many times in my life that I barely trusted my mother and she gave birth to me.

"I will protect you, I will take care of you, and I may learn to love you, but you are asking for more than I can give right now," I told her through gritted teeth but never stopped my stroke. Most of that was the truth. The only thing I had lied about was learning to love her. Pressure had me fucked up in the head and chest, I cared about her a lot. As much as I knew it was love, I didn't want it to be; a man in love was a weak ass man in these streets. I had to be able to drop everything and move if I needed to. I knew I was feeling something strong for her because if I hadn't, she would have been dead a long time ago.

I felt myself about to bust and didn't want to, so I pulled out of her, taking a few breaths before sliding back into her. I bit down on my lip when she took control and started throwing her ass back on me. Pressure was not letting up and as much as I wanted to keep this going, she wasn't going to allow me to. I grabbed her by her hips and plowed into her increasing my speed, but before I got mines, I had to give her another one.

I pulled out of her jagging off and she turned around and caught it in her mouth and continued sucking making me go weak in the knees. When she finally let my dick go her mouth made a popping noise.

"I forgive you," she said, getting up going to the bathroom.

15

RILEY

I replayed the words that I had told Is over in my head as we pulled up to this huge compound right off the ocean in Puerto Plata. I had forgiven him for wanting to take my life for something I had nothing to do with. Since, I had been really questioning my sanity, love really was blind if I was okay with what he had told me. My mother had told me there would come a day that I regretted fucking with Curtis. Although, I regretted that shit for the last ten years I had lived to tell the story. Israel wasn't going to give me a chance to tell the story of falling in love with a man during a fling. He was ready to kill me.

I wanted so much to hate him for telling me the truth that I asked for, but I respected him more than ever. I wanted to hate him for wanting to kill me over something someone else did to him, but as crazy as it may sound, I understood it. This was how the game goes; it was cold, but it was fair.

"What's on your mind?" Is asked me a question that he asked me all the time when I was in deep thought.

"You," I told him honestly.

"What about me?" he asked.

"You just seem like you have a lot of components to you and I'm trying to figure it out," I told him honestly.

"I'm a simple man once you really get to know me, Pressure." He pulled me close to him and kissed the top of my forehead.

"When will that be?" I asked, wondering when would he allow me to really get to know him. I wanted him more than I wanted anything in my life, but I didn't want to bite off more than I could chew. I was tired of everything being so hard, and I wasn't able to have a glimpse of happiness until I met him. Now it was starting to seem like what was simple and easy before wasn't that easy. I still didn't know what part of the streets Israel played in and how it was connected to Curtis. It was so many things I wanted to know but if I knew nothing else, I knew that once I got information, there was no turning back.

"Listen Pressure, let's enjoy our time out here with each other and we'll figure out the rest when we get back to the states." I nodded my head at him.

We walked into the mansion he had rented for us and all I could think was he was showing out. *Who needed a house this big for two people?* I thought to myself but when I walked to the back of the house where the pool was, I got why we were here. The entire back of the house was set up like an oasis. There was a huge pool with a rock waterfall, trees surround the back like we were in a hidden area in the jungle. The jacuzzi was big enough to fit at least six people. There was a stainless-steel kitchen area with everything that you would need to have a day outside grilling, and the bar was fully stocked. When you walked a past all of this there was a man-made rock stream going around most of the back that led to a pond full of Koi fish. As I was taking in everything about the back of the house, Israel grabbed my hand and walked me out the back gate and my feet touched the sand. The ocean was one of the most beautiful things I had seen.

"You like it?" he asked, wrapping and arm around my waist.

"I love it!" I told him, trying to take in everything my eyes landed on.

The Dominican Republic was nothing short of amazing, getting to chill with the people, eating their food, learning the culture, and going out to party. Israel had introduced me to some of his business associates and their wives. When we weren't out in the streets of D.R. we were in the six-bedroom, six-bathroom mansion, or on the beach. These were the type of things I wanted to do in life, just enjoy the fruits of my labor. It made it even better that I could do it with him, he was an amazing man. I was sitting in the bedroom in Chicago, but my mind was still in the Dominican Republic.

"What's good Pressure?" Israel walked up behind me and kissed me on the cheek.

"Nothing much; what's up?"

"I want you to make a run with me, throw on some gym shoes and jeans and meet me in the car." I got up and did as he asked, and we walked out of the door.

When I got to the car, he pulled off without saying anything until we pulled up on a block on the southside; he pulled out a box and handed it to me.

"I need you to take this box, knock on that door where the light is on, give it to the man that opens the door, and he's going to give you an envelope. It should be ten grand in there, all hundreds; count it out in front of him. If it's off, touch the brim of this hat on your way to the car, if it's not, just come get in the car and we out. There doesn't need to be any conversation exchanged, don't even let that nigga know what your voice sound like, you understand?" I stared at him perplexed. I wasn't sure if I should be doing this or not, I had an idea of what was in the box, but I really didn't want to be involved in this shit.

The package was sealed like it had come from FedEx; it didn't seem like it was nothing out of the ordinary. The only problem was the amount of money that I was receiving for it. I had an idea of what it was and what he was asking me to do. I never wanted to be this person. I wanted to be protected from shit like this. I thought about the party that we had went to in the D.R. and how all the men and women we were around looked like they came from old money. One man in particular, everyone surrounded themselves around. The people with him carried guns and Israel had sat at the table talking to him for a while and when they were done, they shook hands and we left.

I began to think about all the old mob and mafia movies that I used to watch, and the shit hit me like a ton of bricks. The same way they moved in the movies was the same way they moved when we were in the D.R. but better.

"What's in it?" I asked him, shaking the box. He turned cold eyes on me, and a chill ran down my spine.

"Does it matter?" was his reply before he frowned his face up at me, snatching the box from me and opened the car door.

"Give it to me I'll do it."

"Naw. I got this." He looked at me with the same frown on his face from before. I reached out to him for the box until he gave it to me.

I took a deep breath trying to figure out why was I putting myself in this position and only one word came to mind: love. I loved him so much I would do anything for him including put my life on the line by busting moves for him. Even with the way he was acting now I still couldn't imagine not doing the things that he had asked me to do for him.

I got out the car and slowly walked to the door, hesitating before I knocked. I looked back at the car and Iss was watching me. It made me feel safe and gave me more courage than I was feeling to knock on the door again. The door opened and a tall, thin, dark-skinned man looked at me then smirked at me before handing me the envelope. He opened the box, pulling out a brick of coke and I counted the money out quickly. It was short fifteen hundred when he opened the door. I walked out, touching the brim of the hat I had on. Iss was already standing outside of the car waiting for me and he began walking towards me.

"Get in the car," he said, walking past me quickly. I turned once I got to the car door only to see Iss holding up his arm and letting off two shots that I barely heard. I paused for a few seconds before getting into the car, not believing what I had just saw. He had just killed a man, right in front of me. I had just caused this to happen, he had no idea how much it was short. What if it was short only ten dollars, he would have lost his life over ten singles? My mind wasn't able to process this shit correctly.

"Why did you do that?" My voice shook as I asked him the question. This was my first time ever seeing someone get killed. I closed my eyes and saw the man's body drop again. When I opened my eyes, Iss was looking at me like he was ready to do the same thing to me too.

"Because this is what I do, this is who I am, you wanted to see me, you wanted to know me right?" I was trying to figure out if I should answer his question or eat what I had just seen.

"Do I need to do your ass too bitch?" he asked me seriously and my eyes got wide as I shook my head no.

"Why would you say that to me? What do you mean this is you? You do this all the time?" I had asked questions that wasn't supposed to come out of my mouth. Iss cocked his head at me like I was crazy.

"What I tell you before, I'll do what I need to, to protect the family. If you not with me Riley that means you against me. Are you with me Riley?" His eyes were pleading with me to not make him do my ass.

16

ISRAEL

I watched Pressure from the corner of my eyes hoping I didn't have to pull the trigger on her ass too. If I had to do it, I would but it would hurt me more than I would want it too. She was damn near perfect for me and depending on how she handled this situation I would wife her ass up. She would never have to worry about a thing in her life if she just fucked with me on this. She took a couple of deep breaths before she stared me down.

"Here we go with this killing me shit again Iss, what the fuck is wrong with you?" she raised her voice at me, and it took everything in me not to choke her ass. She either had a death wish or was crazy to yell at a man with a loaded gun.

"Who you yelling at?"

"You nigga! How many times are you going to threaten my fucking life?" I smirked at her.

"I advise you to pipe the fuck down," I told her seriously before I realized her mood was affected by my mood. I waited and gave her a few minutes to calm down before I spoke again.

"Do you think I'm a bad person because of what I just did?" I asked to fill her out.

"No, I feel like you did what you had to do being who you are." I cocked my head at her knowing that she had to be crazy as hell. I had just dropped a nigga in front of her and she was eating it up better than some niggas. I had to call my mama and tell her I found her new daughter in law.

"What I don't understand is why you did it in front of me." I nodded my head at her understanding where she was coming from. Honestly, I could have waited to get at that nigga, I had been known to wait years to get my revenge on muthafuckas. But I needed to see if Pressure could handle the pressure. I knew that nigga would be short when he saw someone other than me at the door. He was the type of nigga that you had to stand on his neck to get your shit and personally I was tired of playing with his ass. My people knew the rules to the game we played, and he had just played with me for the last time.

"Can you handle it Pressure? This is me, all of me, can you love the nigga I'm showing right now like you love the nigga that want to show you the world? Can you sleep next to me at night knowing I do shit like this to make sure the people I care about eat? Can you love a nigga that's going to get back at anyone that cross him? When I say anyone, I mean that shit." I stared at her so she could really let what I was saying sink in.

"Before you agree, this is who you're getting, I do this shit. I will smile and laugh in a muthafucka face knowing I'm about to dead they ass at the right time in the right place. They be laughing at one thing, and I will be laughing at the fact that their time is about to expire at my hands because of what they have done to me."

"So, everyone that has crossed you, you've killed?" she asked, and I cut my eyes at her.

"The nigga I came up off of over ten years ago is the only muthafucka that ever crossed me and survived. Now that I know he's alive, even that bitch got a deadline too," I told her, staring in her eyes.

She cut her eyes at me, and I could see her holding in every emotion that she was feeling. She had caught on to what I was saying, and I thought I was going to have to take her out after that. I felt myself reaching for the gun and stopped when a tear rolled down her face. I wanted her to apply pressure and she was doing it to me. She had me compromising myself. I never hesitated to take care of business until now, I just hoped I didn't regret my decision.

I pulled up to the house and Riley got out of the car, slamming the door behind her before rushing in the condo. I slowly got out of the car because I wasn't running behind any bitch, including her. A pain hit in my chest when I thought about what I was going to have to do to her. When I got in the house, she was packing her bags. *You really being a soft ass nigga.* I said to myself when I begin to text Trig to handle her for me.

"Where you think you're going?" I watched her toss shit I bought her into one of the big ass Louis Vuitton suitcases. If I was a petty nigga, I would be telling her leave with she came in on her back. Since I had thrown that away she would be walking out of here the way she came into the world, naked. I smirk at the fact that she felt like she would be walking away, she saw what I had done. If I let her go, she would be a liability to my operation, and I didn't believe in having liabilities.

"I'm getting away from your ass." Six words that hurt my ass to the core. I had fell in love with a bitch that couldn't handle who I was. She swore she loved me but couldn't take the man that the streets had made me. I stepped back because I didn't expect to feel the pain that I was feeling over her. Her harsh words impacted me in a way I never thought they would. I know I'm a man, but did she not think that I fucking had feelings? She thought I didn't cry on the inside. She had no idea I turned bottles up to deal with my demons and emotions that I felt.

I used liquor to numb myself from my thoughts and emotions. I walked out of the room we shared to my bar and picked up a fresh bottle of Remi XO. Today was a special occasion and I needed a special type of liquor. Today was the day that I had let a bitch in, and she couldn't hold it together for me. Now I had to hold it down for me and my team.

I walked back in the room with the bottle to my lips taking a gulp. I handed it to her, and she gave me that look that women around the world had mastered. That stank ass look when they look you up and down then flare their nose up, basically telling you to get the fuck on.

"Is it poison?" She asked seriously and I cocked my head at her, giving her a bitch please expression and stance. The bitch had to be out of her mind to think I was about to do my damn self instead of her. I offered the bottle to her again without words and she took it, taking a sip and going back to her task at hand.

"Why are you leaving?" I asked her calmly, trying to see where her mind was at.

"You are seriously asking me this?" She questioned, throwing more shit into the suitcase before walking up to me.

"I asked you, didn't I?" She got all the way up in my face, she was way too close to me for her to be so hostile, but I let her have the floor.

"Do you have any idea what I have been through these last ten years?" She spaced her feet apart and put her hands on her hips. I didn't say anything. I just stared at her frame and stance, ready for whatever she thought she was about to do.

"Hold that thought," I told her walking out of the room and placing my gun in the safe. I knew how my anger was set up and if she tried to put her hands on me, I didn't want to kill her. I walked back into the room to her turning the bottle up and shook my head. I was turning her into me when it came to the alcohol. I walked up and grabbed the bottle from her.

"Do you have any idea what I have been through these last ten years?" She started again where she left off, but this time she wasn't in my face.

"Stop with all the fucking questions, talk to me, I'll listen," I told her, getting tired of the all the questions. She cocked her head, and I knew it was because I was being an asshole, but she was taking me there. I wanted her to open her mouth so I could see where her mind was at, but she was beating around the bush.

"Talk!" I demanded and instead of talking she cried. It was like a dam broke inside of her. She turned her back to me, like she was too strong to let the next motherfucka see her break down. Pressure squatted down and covered her mouth to the gut wrenching cries at bay; her body shook. I walked over to her slowly, not sure what to do, but I knew I couldn't just stand and watch her like this. For her I was humble, for her I was soft, so when I bent down to hold her, I didn't expect her to jump out of the way.

"You fucked up my life." I bounced up off the floor like I had springs in my legs. I wasn't about to play this angry black woman shit with her ass. I knew what a mad bitch could do to an unexpecting nigga, and I didn't want no parts of what she had going on.

"Girl I ain't did shit to you." I told her, giving her some space. I wasn't scared of her, but I didn't want to hurt her either. So, I backed up and watched the lioness on the prowl.

"You did this to me; I have been through so much and it's all at your fucking hands. How could you make me love you? Putting me through all these test and shit and you knew you were the reason my life had been a living fucking hell."

"What the fuck are you talking about, shorty?" I asked because I knew she had me confused with someone else. Yeah, I had tested her ass and she pass that shit with flying colors each time. The only time she let me down was tonight.

"Now that I think about that party in the Dominican Republic, some of those niggas were at my fucking wedding. It had been so long since I had seen them that I hadn't even remembered until now. Until I found out that you were the one that tried to kill Curtis. You fucked up my life over a connect nigga."

I was starting to feel uneasy at how she said I tried to kill Curtis; was she out here fucking with me and still in love with this nigga?

"Okay," I told her and laughed in my head when her facial expression changed. This was a serious matter, and I should have been taking it that way, but I had a fucked-up sense of humor. When Riley saw the smirk on my face, she went crazy, she picked up a bottle of perfume I had gotten her and threw it at me. *At least she was fucking up her own shit.* I thought and ended up laughing out loud and causing her to try and fuck me up.

I wrapped her ass up in my arms, pinning her down to the bed, seeing this much fight in her had my dick hard as hell. I knew she had this in her. Pressure was on attack mode. The only problem was that she wanted to release her wrath on me.

"You not about to think you can whip my ass in here. I won't put my hands on you, but I will choke he fuck out of you, Riley. Calm the fuck down!" I raised my voice at her letting her know I wasn't about to play these goofy ass games with her.

"Just let me leave." Her eyes pleaded with me, but I couldn't do that.

"Hell naw, sit in this muthafucka and think about how you been acting and why. This is the only chance you will ever get from me Riley and I'm taking a big one on you. You always ask me to trust you, by not dropping your ass right now, I'm putting my trust in you. Bitch, I'm putting my fucking life in your hands. I don't trust my life with anyone but myself."

"Fuck your life nigga, you didn't care about mines." She retorted and I wrapped my hand around her neck, applying just a little pressure to it.

"I'm a forget you said that and let you think this over." I kissed her on her cheek, got off of her and walked out of the room, locking the door behind me. I couldn't wait until she tried to open the door and leave. I had to show Riley it was my way or no way at all, her ass would be in that room for a year if that's what it took for her to act right.

I turned the cellphone jammer on in the house and walked out, I had shit to do.

17

ISRAEL

"I know I had thoughts of locking Honey ass up in the house when we first met, but damn nigga you really did that to her." Trig laughed so hard at me, he was holding his stomach. I, on the other hand, didn't see shit funny. I thought I had found the right woman for me, but I had failed. Pressure was everything good in this world with a big ass heart, it fucked me up because I knew if nothing else, I was a good ass judge of character. So how did I fuck up so bad with her?

"Nigga this ain't funny." I pushed his ass with my elbow because he was laughing a little too hard at my expense. Me doing that only made him laugh harder because he didn't give a fuck. To him, I was his little brother and brothers got down on each other all the time.

"Whatever you say bruh, but for real, how's it going?" I shrugged my shoulders at him.

"This whole time I thought she was mad and popping her shit because I'm a damn killer and I was at Curtis's head." I paused and he looked at me, waiting for me to continue. I thought back to the other day when I finally went into the room to talk to Riley. She hadn't been feeling too good and I wanted to see where her mind was at. She had been in there for about a week, I made sure she had everything she needed in there. She had three square meals a day with all her favorite snacks, water, juice and pop.

I walked into the room once I heard her in the bathroom throwing up.

"Pressure you cool?" I asked her with a bowl of soup in my hand for her.

"Yeah, I just don't feel too good," she told me and walked out of the bathroom after brushing her teeth and washing her face. She walked to the bed and laid down, taking a deep breath. She had been in this room for over a week, but baby girl looked exhausted. I hated seeing her like this because usually she was upbeat and ready to do everything. Even the other days of her being locked in the room she still had a little spunk to her even though she wasn't fucking with me like that.

"I don't feel like the back and forth today Iss, I just want some sleep." She told me, conceding to any of the bullshit I had up my sleeve.

"You good Pressure, I just need you to eat something," I told her handing the bowl of soup I had made for her when I heard her throwing up earlier. She nodded her head and sat up in the bed, eating the soup slowly like she was doing everything in her power to hold it down. After taking a few bites of it she sat the bowl to the side and laid down. I couldn't help lying next to her and pulling her close to me. I hadn't touched her in over a week and the shit was driving me crazy. I thought she would pull away from me, but she didn't. She got even closer to me, laying her head on my chest.

"I don't like this Iss," she said talking into my chest.

"I'm a make sure I get you better," I told her seriously, if nothing else she should know I cared about her health.

"Not me being sick, us like this. You locking me in this room, you staying away from me like I have a contagious disease or something." If she only knew when it came to her and me, she was like the black plague. Her ass was making me feel things that a nigga like me didn't ever want to feel. She was making me want more when I have never wanted more.

"What do you want from me, Riley?" I asked her. She pulled back a little and looked me in my eyes for a few minutes before she spoke.

"You!" she told me honestly. I was shocked, she had done all that shit the other day, had me ready to kill her and she wanted me. It sounded so good to me, but could I trust her? I had been known to tell people for years what they wanted to hear just to get my way. Was she doing the same thing to me?

"If you can handle a nigga like me, why all that shit the other day then?" She kept her eyes on mines and licked her lips before she spoke.

"I was hurt, I felt betrayed by you." She paused, and I let her collect her thoughts without interrupting her. This was her time to talk, and I was going to give her the floor no matter how long it took her to get it out.

"I need you to understand that those ten years of my life was pure hell. I was eighteen when Curtis got shot and we were fresh into marriage. Although I was young, everything that I said in front of everyone was true at the time. I meant in sickness and in health and for richer or poorer until death do us part. I had no idea that the sickness would come so soon, I was trying to be loyal. For ten years I wiped ass, cleaned up after him, cleaned him up, changed his sheets, clothes, and fed him. For ten years I was a slave to and for him while he called me stupid, threw whatever he could get his hands on at me and even put his hands on me. I lost myself with him, I couldn't tell who I was. I lost my friends and family trying to take care of a man that hated me because I was able to walk around. I let him fuck my head up calling me ugly and fat, telling me I won't be shit because I was a reflection of him. I let him tear me down because I thought that's what a good wife does for her husband. Until I met you." Everything that she was telling me only made me want to kill this nigga even more. Who the fuck was he to try and break my bitch? That explains her looking fucked up in the store that day, but I could still see the potential in her then.

"Damn Pressure."

"I was mad at you because I felt like this is as much as your fault as it was mines. I was stupid for staying, but you were stupid for not making sure the job was finished before you walked off. I was mad at you too because if we are going to be fucking around you can't hide shit like this from me Iss." I kissed her on her forehead.

"The less you know the better," I told her and she rolled her eyes.

"Seriously Riley I have to protect you," I told her.

"From who, you? You're the only one that has the ability to hurt me Iss. You helped build me back up and helped me see the potential I have in myself as a woman. You were the one that told me it's my world and when a muthafucka steps into my world they have to acknowledge me. They have to realize in my shit, I apply the pressure, and that I'm welcoming them under my sunrays. You helped boss me up mentally and I don't give a fuck what you have going on I just want you." I smirked when she told me that because I did tell her all of that and more. Baby girl was processing the knowledge I dropped on her and utilizing it too. It wasn't a bitch in a room that could fuck with her because I made sure she knew she was the shit. The bitch could be the prettiest in the world and still couldn't hold a candle to Pressure because I had built her mentally. I had gotten in her head to turn her into the bossed-up ass female I knew she could be.

"What about all the other shit?" I asked her, just to make sure we were on the same page.

"Nigga I don't give a fuck who you kill as long as you make it back home to me." I nodded my head at her because she was built strong and I had nothing to do with it, life had made he that way. It was a shame she didn't see herself like I saw her.

"It wasn't that?" Trig asked me and frowned when it took me a minute to answer him. I shook my head no at him.

"She was mad over some other shit, but we got that together."

"When you going to let her out the room?" he asked, laughing a little.

"I don't know man; you know I don't trust nobody and it's hard for me to trust her with my life. What if she on some get back shit? I wasted ten years of her life so now she gone do the same to me."

"First off nigga you're not dumb; what she saw you do carry's a life sentence. Next off, you have to start somewhere, just put one of the boys on her to follow her." I nodded my head because Trig always brought clarity to situations.

❧

"I need to get out of here; I've been in this room for damn near two weeks." I watched Pressure pace the floor and I knew she was about to go stir crazy. She was pulling at her long curly hair like she was trying to snatch it out of her head.

"I really hate to see you like this," I told her. I know what Trig had told me, but I was still skeptical about letting her out of my sight.

"Israel this is worse than the prison I was in with Curtis, at least I had a whole house to be in and freedom to go to the store. I was able to go out get me some weed and buy my own shit. You are holding me captive and I'm about to lose my shit. I want to get out, get some fresh air, talk to people, you know do things that people do." What she said just made me feel like shit, I knew I was holding her here but damn. Prison? I was worse than the nigga that was beating her ass.

18

RILEY

"What I'm not enough for you?" Israel asked and I was ready to go upside his shit. He had me locked in this room for damn near two weeks. I had been in here fighting demons wanting more from a nigga that may be incapable of loving and trusting me the way I love and trust him. I thought when I saw him pull the trigger on that man that I would have nightmares about it. I thought that I would wake in the middle of the night screaming at the top of my lungs because I had seen something that was supposed to be so traumatic. I thought that every time I closed my eyes, I would see his limp ass body drop to the ground, and the smirk that Israel wore fade into the background. I thought I would be losing it over this and who he was but nope I could care less about that man.

It was sad he had to go, but fuck him. I wanted out of this room. I didn't even care that he had tried to kill Curtis. Iss dropping niggas was the last thing on my mind.

"Am I not enough for you?" Israel asked again snapping his fingers in my face. I blinked a few times because it was just like a nigga to think everything was about him. This shit was about me and how I was handling things in my head. I was in this room sick and fucking depressed.

"This has nothing to do with you or that nigga that you murked, or Curtis. You are more than enough for me, but I want the same freedoms that you have. I want to come and go as I please, I want to make my own fucking meals Iss." he nodded his head, and I paced the floor.

Life was beating my ass in this room, I knew I had given up a lot fucking with Curtis, but I started to realize time wasn't the only thing I had given up. Time was precious but I had lost a lot of other things along the way too. Like my will, self-respect, courage, drive and ambition. I had really lost who I was with him and now Israel was in this muthafucka trying to make me lose my mind. At least he would help me find it afterwards. Curtis didn't give a fuck.

"Pressure," Israel called my name and I turned to him. I knew I was in this room because he didn't trust me, but he didn't know that I would end my own life before I traded on him. I wasn't even mad at him anymore, I just wanted out of this damn twenty feet by twenty uncomfortable ass cell he had me in.

"Get dressed, we going out tonight, it's Honey's birthday." I didn't fuck with Honey to tough and I knew it was because she was a good friend of Ziyah's. At this point I didn't give a fuck I jumped up and down because my thick ass was about to leave this room. It wasn't shit that could ruin my mood as of right now. I went to the closet and pulled out a couple of outfits to try on, when Israel left the room, I turned around to make sure the door was still open.

I had to be crazy to still love the nigga that held me hostage in his damn bedroom. My heart did a double beat as I pulled out some shoes and decided that I was crazy as hell.

I stepped out of the all black metallic Lamborghini truck with black and red rims like I owned the club that we were going into. Israel grabbed my hand as soon as my black and red, red bottom sandal hit the pavement. Since it was Honey's birthday, I decided to do a simple black bodycon halter dress that hugged all the right places. I didn't have a lot time to pull everything together, so I pulled my hair into a sleek ponytail and let my curls hang.

Israel wasted no time taking me right to the V.I.P. section where Trig, Honey, Ziyah, and some other people were sitting.

"Riley this is Bones, Lucky, and Draco; y'all this my girl Riley." Israel introduced us and avoided telling me who the women they were with were. I guess they didn't matter, so I didn't press it just nodded my head at them after I spoke to the fellas. When we walked to the spot Trig, Honey and Ziyah were sitting Ziyah rolled her eyes at me, and I smiled.

"I'm sure she won't remember who's who; it's not like she gets the picture when it comes to shit," Ziyah said and laughed at her own joke. *I'm really going to have to put my foot in this bitch mouth sooner or later.* I thought to myself as I smiled at her and sat in Israel's lap. *Laugh at that bitch.* I thought when her face dropped, and she rolled her eyes. Israel wrapped an arm around my waist and readjusted me on his lap so he could see.

Honey noticed the change in the atmosphere and grabbed Ziyah by her hand pulling her away from us so they could dance. Ziyah gave the evil eyes all the way to the dance floor. I picked up my glass of water toasting it to her. She flipped me the bird and Israel hit me on the thigh.

"Stop that shit, you better than that." As the words left his mouth, I wanted to tell him no I wasn't. I hated for bitches like her to come at me, I personally hadn't done anything to her. It wasn't my fault we loved the same man, and it wasn't my fault that she couldn't get over it. I was smart enough to not put anything past these niggas they literally would tell a female what they wanted to hear. I wasn't sure what her and Iss past was, but as of right now I was his present. If there ever came a time that I wasn't with him, I wouldn't tear the next bitch down I would wish her well because he was a lot to deal with.

"Why you not drinking?" Israel asked and I shrugged at him.

"I'm not in a big liquor mood tonight. My stomach has just settled from the other day." He put his glass up to my lips trying to get me to take a sip and I shook my head.

"Just a little. Baby," he told me, and I shook my head no to him again.

"No Is, I just want to chill tonight, enjoy yourself and I'll drive us home later," I said, hoping it would satisfy him enough to not push the issue.

"What was the point of us coming out for this if you're not going to join in the festivities? We could have stayed at home." I rolled my eyes at him; I swear this nigga had multiple personalities or something.

"I'm good on that, baby. I don't want to get sick again," I told him honestly.

"Iss, I don't think you should push the issue," Trig told him and I damn near hugged the nigga for looking out.

"There isn't an issue man, one drink ain't gone fuck with her." Iss told him and Trig shook his head. Israel tried to hand me another drink and I told him no getting off his lap. This shit was starting to get stupid to me and at this point all I wanted to do was leave. I would have asked the nigga if he was drunk but the XO that he took down before we left the house and the cup that he had drank since we got here was enough for me to know. Usually, he was a happy ass drunk that would give anyone anything without question, but tonight he was being an asshole.

I got off of his lap and walked out of the club. I was about to catch an Uber back to the house. Shit, he could lock me back in the room if he was going to be acting like this when we were out in public. I stood at the curb, waiting for my ride to show up.

"Trouble in paradise?" Ziyah's voice came from nowhere.

"Bitch mind your business! Shouldn't you be in there tossing that little ass around for my man to see." I asked her with venom in my voice. I didn't have time for her ass, and I felt like I was getting dizzy. All I wanted to do was go home and go to sleep, but she was stopping me, and her perfume was doing a number on me.

"His business is my business." She told me with confidence, stepping in my face.

"Move back," I told her trying to hold the contents of my stomach in, but she wasn't allowing me too.

"I ain't moving shit." She got closer and everything I had ate came up and out on her shoes and legs. *I bet the bitch will listen next time.* I thought to myself while I smirked at her.

"What the fuck is going on out here?" I didn't say a word, just shook my head at him. He finally turned around once Ziyah screamed like someone was murdering her. She ran towards us and Iss pushed her back with a disgusted expression on his face.

"Riley what the fuck is going on?" he asked, staring at me.

"Iss, I think I'm pregnant," I told him, and he stepped away from me.

"Naw, that ain't a good look." He told me acting like he couldn't be around me.

"What the fuck is that supposed to mean?" I asked him ready to have the battle of a lifetime out here in front of all these people.

"I don't want any kids Pressure; you have to get rid of it if you are," he told me, shaking his head no to me. Trig and Honey came outside standing around us.

"Pregnant, she's fucking pregnant!" Ziyah yelled like the news of me being pregnant cut her to the core. Iss truck was brought around and parked in front of us.

"How could you do this to me? You allowed this bitch to get pregnant and every time I got pregnant you made me abort it? What's so good about her that she can still be pregnant, and I couldn't. Nigga you knew my period schedule better than I knew my own. If I was late more than two days, you were carrying me to the hospital getting me an ultrasound." Ziyah was cracking in front of all of us.

"Riley, get in the truck." Israel told me and I opened the door to get in.

"Israel, I am your wife!" Ziyah yelled and started towards him like she was ready to drop his ass. Honey jumped in front of Israel trying to keep Ziyah away from him. Trig pulled him back because at that point, Israel seemed like he wanted all the smoke.

I didn't move. I was completely in shock trying to figure out what the hell was going on. I expected Israel to deny what she was saying, but instead he looked like he was mad that she dropped the bomb. From the expressions on Trig and Honey's face they knew nothing about this marriage either. I thought about all the times I had saw him treat this woman like she was a nuisance, like she didn't matter to him, but they were married.

The other shoe had dropped. I could deal with him being a drug dealer, a killer in these streets, but being married to a woman and treating her how he treated Ziyah was a no go for me. She walked around like she had rights to him because she did. Legally, he belonged to her, and I was the woman in the wrong. All those times he spoke about trusting me and I couldn't trust him to tell me the truth about something as simple as being married. Ziyah walked around like a lovesick puppy behind Israel and she had the right to.

I stood back and watched the drama unfold, Ziyah kicked and screamed as she tried to attack Israel. Who was I to step in the middle of a husband and wife's fight? Hell, I was the side chick that didn't even know she was the side chick. I had been lied to, tricked, and handled. My emotions were getting the best of me, and I wanted to pull Ziyah from Honey's arms and we both could beat Israel's ass. I wanted to jump all over him kicking, screaming, and yelling. He saved me, only to destroy me, only to pop me off, tell me I can't have it, fuck me good, and leave me.

"Get on the driver's side, Riley," Trig told me and when I moved from the door to go around the truck a shot rang out and we all hit the ground.

19

TRIG

"This is all my fault; this is all my fault." Honey repeated to herself as Riley hit one hundred miles per hour to make it to the hospital. I looked in the back seat at her trying to figure out what the fuck was she talking about. I know she didn't feel like this was on her because we were out here for her birthday.

"This isn't on you Honey, this shit could have happened anywhere at any time. You know how this game goes," I said, hoping it would help.

"It's not your fault Honey, I shouldn't have been outside arguing with him." Riley stated and I looked at her.

"This shit ain't on you either, Israel know how these streets is. He should have just got in the truck and took you home instead of standing out there arguing with muthafuckas," I told both of them seriously. I wasn't high enough to deal with two females in the car blaming themselves for something that they probably had nothing to do with.

"Naw you don't understand," Honey told me.

"Well help me understand," I replied, and she looked me in my eyes. I knew we would be having a conversation once we saw what was going on with Iss. Whatever was going on with her, I needed the truth and not that shit she been trying to give me these last few months. The person that was sitting in this back seat breaking down wasn't her. She took shit like this like a real nigga. Yeah, we fucked up because he is one of our own, but he ain't dead; he is a fighter, and I knew he would make it through this. Why she didn't have that same mentality at this moment was beyond me. Riley was sitting here taking this situation better than her and she was fucking him.

"We'll talk," Honey said defeated. I nodded my head at her and pulled out my pre rolled blunt to calm my nerves. Between these two and the fact that Israel was hit in the chest had me on edge. I was ready to go out and paint the city red over my brother, but before I did that, I had to make sure he was cool. All I had in this world was him and Honey and they both kept me as sane as I could possibly be.

I hit my blunt and thought about how everything went down, Israel being drunk and getting out of his body. Riley being pregnant and Ziyah and Israel being married. I knew they were fucking around, but they were married, and they hid it well. No one had lived with Israel until Riley came along so all of this was a shock to me. I looked at Riley and watched the tears roll down her face. I had to give it to her. She was handling this better than I expected. Ziyah didn't want to get in the truck with us which was understandable since she had to go home and clean up.

All of us was covered in his blood trying to make sure we kept him alive. Ziyah on the other hand stood back like she had become shell shocked. She didn't drop a tear or utter a word until he was being put in the ambulance. I guess something in her mind clicked that it was Israel trying to hold on to his life.

Riley pulled up to the hospital burning rubber to stop the truck and we all hopped out.

"Shit, we should've brought him ourselves." Honey stated as the ambulance he was in pulled up behind us. They rushed him in the hospital, and we were on their heels until they blocked us off from getting to the back.

I watched Riley pace the floors and Honey sit in the corner by herself with her eyes closed. Her eyebrows were furrowed together like she was stressing hard. I thought about her statement in the car and walked over to her.

"I done came to you a couple times about what's fucking with you. You always have some type of excuse or game to run on me. I'm not asking you now, I'm telling you, give it to me raw." Honey opened her eyes and stared at me for a minute. I knew it was a fucked-up time for me to ask her about this, but we needed to put the situation to rest.

"Israel getting shot is my fault." She told me for the hundredth time and paused.

"This is my last time telling you to let me know what's going on. I can't do shit about the situation if I don't know what's going on." My words came out harsh, but she knew I wasn't the type of nigga to have muthafuckas beating around the bush with me. Honey sat there like I hadn't said a word. She stared across the room for so long I snapped my fingers in front of her face to get her attention.

"Someone has been stalking me since we got back from Miami." My back stiffened at her words. I had so many questions but only one stood out in the front of my brain right now.

"What does this have to do with Iss getting shot?" I asked her, already knowing the answer to my own question. She stared at me and pursed her lips before looking around to make sure no one was close enough to hear us.

"I think they were trying to kill me. Think about it. I had just moved from in front of him when the shot rang out." I stared at her because Honey and I had done so much dirt together there was no telling who was after her. We made sure we tied up our loose ends but there was always a chance that one of their people would come back to retaliate. I needed more information like why in the fuck hadn't she been dropped this?

"Tell me everything." My voice was cold with her, and her eyes widened after I spoke. Although I was pissed off at her, I was more pissed that someone was coming after what was mines. Most muthafuckas in the streets knew not to come my way and that included fucking with her.

I sat back and listened to her as she told me how her and her father used to do hits. He would always leave a black rose to torment his next victim. We had been together for years and she never told me that her father was X. I couldn't be mad at her because I had a past that I never talked about too. Some shit just didn't need to be exposed because you never knew who your enemies were or would be. X was a legend and not just in the city of Chicago, if you had a problem that seemed impossible, he was the one called. Knowing who her father was explained a lot about her and it explained why she didn't tell me from jump. X had done so much during his time it could be anyone around the world that was coming for her.

I took in everything she was saying, knowing I was going to have to have my people behind me to deal with this situation. I asked her did she have anyone in mind and what she had done so far to see who was behind this.

"I have nothing, Trig." I nodded my head at her and stood up. I had to leave. The hospital was not the place for me to be after getting all this information. My brother was here fighting for his life and my girl might be next on the list.

"I'll be back." I walked out of the waiting room. I needed to clear my head and get a plan in motion. I wasn't about to leave the hospital, but I had to make some calls to some of my contacts. There wasn't anything I could do for Iss just sitting in there, but I could make some progress by putting niggas ears to the streets.

I got to the truck that was sitting in front of the emergency entrance and was glad it hadn't been towed. I went to the driver side of the truck to move it and paused when I opened the door, and a black rose was sitting in the seat. I put my hand on my gun and checked my surroundings. My eyes landed on damn near every vehicle that was close to me before I got comfortable enough to get in the truck. I tossed the rose out of the window and pulled off.

20

RILEY

I sat in the back room on an emotional rollercoaster. I was feeling so many things at one time that I thought I was about to break. I had to hold myself together because I had no one here that would have me if I went down. Israel was in surgery fighting for his life. I knew that he would be okay because that nigga was a fighter. I couldn't help but to think of all the things that had went on within a matter of minutes. All it took was minutes for everything to go to hell.

I looked at the papers that the nurse had given me after I checked myself in saying that my stomach was hurting. The first thing they did was give me a pregnancy test which was positive. The picture of the little sac and pea sat on the table next to my discharge papers. I was supposed to be out of this room thirty minutes ago, but I was stuck here in my own thoughts. Tears rolled down my face when I replayed the way Israel looked at me when I told him I thought I was pregnant. *"Get rid of it, I don't want it."* His words ripped through me because how could you show me you love me but can't love what our love created?

I wanted to run away, just leave while he was here and he couldn't stop me, but I couldn't. Loyalty again kept me from leaving, I had to make sure he was good. If he left this world today, I would want to be able to tell our child I was here with him to the end. If he didn't, I wanted to be able to let our child know we would go to daddy when the time was right. One thing I knew was that I wasn't going to get rid of a child that would love me unconditionally.

Then, it was that entire matter of him being married to Ziyah. Israel was the love that I didn't know I wanted and needed, he was my good time, he helped keep me sane. Israel was the love of my life only for me to find out that he wasn't shit.

I was trying to figure out how a man so loving and giving to the woman that he was with could still be an ain't shit nigga. My heart was breaking as I thought about him and Ziyah going back and forth with each other. I told myself I was strong enough to walk away, I had done it with Curtis after ten years. It shouldn't be nothing for me to walk away from Is, and not look back. As the thought crossed my mind my heart was breaking, but I had to do this for my child. There was no telling what Ziyah was capable of, she loved him just as much as I did if not more. She had abortion after abortion just to keep him and for him to treat her like she didn't matter. Like she wasn't his wife, like she hadn't given up so much.

Israel was selfish, and as much as I loved him, I couldn't be with someone that wouldn't give me just as much as I gave him. I didn't need his money. I could make it on my own, I could hold myself down. My child and I would be good out here on our own. I just didn't know how I was going to be able to live with the heartbreak. He had broken barriers in me getting to my heart that I thought was so cold after not being loved for years. I had no other choice but to walk away and the knowledge of that was killing me.

I took a deep breath collecting my things holding everything I had close to me. As I walked down the hall, my skin felt sticky from being covered in Israel's blood. The nurse that took care of me had given me some doctors scrubs to put on to change out of my bloody clothes, but it didn't matter. His blood was all over me, it was sinking deep into my pores like he had sunk into my heart.

"You okay?" Honey asked in a soft voice when I walked back into the waiting room. I nodded my head yes to her because if I spoke, she would hear nothing but pain in my voice. I held my head back and pinched the bridge of my nose to keep the tears from falling.

"He's going to be good; I know it." I stared at her because out of all the time we had been around each other we had never really held a conversation. She walked around with this hard exterior and a don't fuck with me attitude. This was the first time that I saw her as a woman with femininity and not a cold-hearted ass bitch. I got it though, they didn't know me. They were his and Ziyah's people; they were their friends and I had stepped into their world with him. They owed me nothing, not even a hello in the streets.

"I know," was my reply as I went to sit down on the other side of the waiting room. I wasn't trying to be rude, but I wasn't trying to build bonds over sadness either. I needed just as much space as she had given me when we were around each other outside of here. I leaned my head on the wall and closed my eyes.

"Wake up, they said you can go back to see Iss." Honey shook me until my eyes popped open.

"He made it." I responded, exhaling a breath and she nodded her head at me smiling.

"I'm calling Trigg now, only two people can go back and since Ziyah hasn't gotten here yet I think it should be you two. Go ahead, I'll be in the OR waiting room." I nodded my head smiling.

Although I was mad at him and was leaving in the morning, I couldn't help being happy that he had made it through. At least I could see him one last time before I go.

I walked into his room nervous, he had cords and wires everywhere. His breathing was steady though, he looked like he was sleeping. I let my eyes roam over every inch of him trying to commit it to memory. I kissed his lips softly then sat in the chair next to the bed and held his hand in mines. *I can't do this.* I thought to myself. I had to get him to understand that there was no way I was getting rid of my child. My chest tightened at the thought of not seeing him again after this. This couldn't be our last goodbye; I wasn't about to let it.

"Mmm..." he moaned, and I stood up.

"I'm right here, baby. I'm not going anywhere I promise," I told, him squeezing his hand a little. His eyes popped open, and he shook his head at me, lifting the hand that I wasn't holding. It was then I noticed the handcuff that was on his left hand, and it was attached to the bed. I looked around trying to figure out what the fuck was going on. I knew I wasn't in that much of a daze walking in here that I hadn't saw the police.

"Let my fucking hand go bitch, you set me up." Israel yelled at me with his eyes wild like he believed everything that he was saying.

"What are you talking about? What's going on? I don't understand." My questions were coming out quick.

"Fuck that, don't try and play that innocent shit now, I saw that nigga. Curtis was at this door sitting in his wheelchair smirking at me. Right after that, the fucking police came and put cuffs on me. Bitch, I'm at your head, there's nowhere you will be able to hide. On my unborn kids you a dead bitch." Every word that came out of his mouth cut me so deep, that I couldn't even function enough to communicate my thoughts.

"I would never do that." I spoke through my tears. I would never Israel, we have a baby on the way," I told him, wanting him to understand that my loyalty to him overshadowed everything else.

"Bitch fuck that baby. I'ma drop your ass." He said that shit with so much emotion I felt it as the police came in the room pushing me out. Israel lifted the hand I had been holding and pointed at me like a gun.

"I have no idea how she got past us." One of the cops in the hallway was explaining.

"Israel!" I yelled out at him as all of his monitors started going crazy. Nurses and doctors rushed into his room as I tried to push pass the officers that had me to get to him. This shit can't be happening, he can't leave me like this.

"Clear!" someone in the room yelled and they shocked him with the paddles. The sound of the long beep that was coming from the room never wavered.

"Clear!" they yelled again then a third time. I held my breath, hoping for the best until I heard someone yell.

"Call it!" I stopped listening to everything around me. I was lost in my own thoughts, gone into my own world.

"Riley, we have to get out of here." I blinked back my tears. Honey was standing in front of me holding a black rose in her hand. I turned around with her holding tight to my hand dragging me through the hospital. It took me a minute to realize what was happening, the three men I had met at the club and Trig were being arrested right in front of me. I slowed my pace, stopping in my tracks realizing what was really going on. I had lost him, and he thought I was responsible for this.

"Israel no!" I yelled, dropping to my knees.

TO BE CONTINUED...